When Shadows Fall

SELECTED FICTION WORKS BY L. RON HUBBARD

FANTASY

The Case of the Friendly Corpse
Death's Deputy
Fear
The Ghoul
The Indigestible Triton
Slaves of Sleep & The Masters of Sleep
Typewriter in the Sky
The Ultimate Adventure

SCIENCE FICTION

Battlefield Earth
The Conquest of Space
The End Is Not Yet
Final Blackout
The Kilkenny Cats
The Kingslayer
The Mission Earth Dekalogy*
Ole Doc Methuselah
To the Stars

ADVENTURE

The Hell Job series

WESTERN

Buckskin Brigades
Empty Saddles
Guns of Mark Jardine
Hot Lead Payoff

A full list of L. Ron Hubbard's novellas and short stories is provided at the back.

*Dekalogy—a group of ten volumes

L. RON HUBBARD

WHEN SHADOWS FALL

GALAXY PRESS

Published by
Galaxy Press, LLC
7051 Hollywood Boulevard, Suite 200
Hollywood, CA 90028

Printed in the United States of America.

ISBN-10 1-59212-283-3
ISBN-13 978-1-59212-283-7

Library of Congress Control Number: 2007927675

CONTENTS

FOREWORD	vii
WHEN SHADOWS FALL	1
TOUGH OLD MAN	25
BATTLING BOLTO	63
STORY PREVIEW: ONE WAS STUBBORN	87
GLOSSARY	93
L. RON HUBBARD IN THE GOLDEN AGE OF PULP FICTION	97
THE STORIES FROM THE GOLDEN AGE	109

FOREWORD

Stories from Pulp Fiction's Golden Age

AND it *was* a golden age.

The 1930s and 1940s were a vibrant, seminal time for a gigantic audience of eager readers, probably the largest per capita audience of readers in American history. The magazine racks were chock-full of publications with ragged trims, garish cover art, cheap brown pulp paper, low cover prices—and the most excitement you could hold in your hands.

"Pulp" magazines, named for their rough-cut, pulpwood paper, were a vehicle for more amazing tales than Scheherazade could have told in a million and one nights. Set apart from higher-class "slick" magazines, printed on fancy glossy paper with quality artwork and superior production values, the pulps were for the "rest of us," adventure story after adventure story for people who liked to *read.* Pulp fiction authors were no-holds-barred entertainers—real storytellers. They were more interested in a thrilling plot twist, a horrific villain or a white-knuckle adventure than they were in lavish prose or convoluted metaphors.

The sheer volume of tales released during this wondrous golden age remains unmatched in any other period of literary history—hundreds of thousands of published stories in over nine hundred different magazines. Some titles lasted only an issue or two; many magazines succumbed to paper shortages during World War II, while others endured for decades yet. Pulp fiction remains as a treasure trove of stories you can read, stories you can love, stories you can remember. The stories were driven by plot and character, with grand heroes, terrible villains, beautiful damsels (often in distress), diabolical plots, amazing places, breathless romances. The readers wanted to be taken beyond the mundane, to live adventures far removed from their ordinary lives—and the pulps rarely failed to deliver.

In that regard, pulp fiction stands in the tradition of all memorable literature. For as history has shown, good stories are much more than fancy prose. William Shakespeare, Charles Dickens, Jules Verne, Alexandre Dumas—many of the greatest literary figures wrote their fiction for the readers, not simply literary colleagues and academic admirers. And writers for pulp magazines were no exception. These publications reached an audience that dwarfed the circulations of today's short story magazines. Issues of the pulps were scooped up and read by over thirty million avid readers each month.

Because pulp fiction writers were often paid no more than a cent a word, they had to become prolific or starve. They also had to write aggressively. As Richard Kyle, publisher and editor of *Argosy,* the first and most long-lived of the pulps, so pointedly explained: "The pulp magazine writers, the best of them, worked for markets that did not write for critics or attempt to satisfy timid advertisers. Not having to answer to anyone other than their readers, they wrote about human beings on the edges of the unknown, in those new lands the future would explore. They wrote for what we would become, not for what we had already been."

Some of the more lasting names that graced the pulps include H. P. Lovecraft, Edgar Rice Burroughs, Robert E. Howard, Max Brand, Louis L'Amour, Elmore Leonard, Dashiell Hammett, Raymond Chandler, Erle Stanley Gardner, John D. MacDonald, Ray Bradbury, Isaac Asimov, Robert Heinlein—and, of course, L. Ron Hubbard.

In a word, he was among the most prolific and popular writers of the era. He was also the most enduring—hence this series—and certainly among the most legendary. It all began only months after he first tried his hand at fiction, with L. Ron Hubbard tales appearing in *Thrilling Adventures, Argosy, Five-Novels Monthly, Detective Fiction Weekly, Top-Notch, Texas Ranger, War Birds, Western Stories,* even *Romantic Range.* He could write on any subject, in any genre, from jungle explorers to deep-sea divers, from G-men and gangsters, cowboys and flying aces to mountain climbers, hard-boiled detectives and spies. But he really began to shine when he turned his talent to science fiction and fantasy of which he authored nearly fifty novels or novelettes to forever change the shape of those genres.

Following in the tradition of such famed authors as Herman Melville, Mark Twain, Jack London and Ernest Hemingway, Ron Hubbard actually lived adventures that his own characters would have admired—as an ethnologist among primitive tribes, as prospector and engineer in hostile climes, as a captain of vessels on four oceans. He even wrote a series of articles for *Argosy,* called "Hell Job," in which he lived and told of the most dangerous professions a man could put his hand to.

Finally, and just for good measure, he was also an accomplished photographer, artist, filmmaker, musician and educator. But he was first and foremost a *writer,* and that's the L. Ron Hubbard we come to know through the pages of this volume.

This library of Stories from the Golden Age presents the best of L. Ron Hubbard's fiction from the heyday of storytelling, the Golden Age of the pulp magazines. In these eighty volumes, readers are treated to a full banquet of 153 stories, a kaleidoscope of tales representing every imaginable genre: science fiction, fantasy, western, mystery, thriller, horror, even romance—action of all kinds and in all places.

Because the pulps themselves were printed on such inexpensive paper with high acid content, issues were not meant to endure. As the years go by, the original issues of every pulp from *Argosy* through *Zeppelin Stories* continue crumbling into brittle, brown dust. This library preserves the L. Ron Hubbard tales from that era, presented with a distinctive look that brings back the nostalgic flavor of those times.

L. Ron Hubbard's Stories from the Golden Age has something for every taste, every reader. These tales will return you to a time when fiction was good clean entertainment and the most fun a kid could have on a rainy afternoon or the best thing an adult could enjoy after a long day at work.

Pick up a volume, and remember what reading is supposed to be all about. Remember curling up with a *great story.*

—Kevin J. Anderson

KEVIN J. ANDERSON *is the author of more than ninety critically acclaimed works of speculative fiction, including The Saga of Seven Suns, the continuation of the Dune Chronicles with Brian Herbert, and his* New York Times *bestselling novelization of L. Ron Hubbard's* Ai! Pedrito!

When Shadows Fall

When Shadows Fall

AND then there came a day when Earth lay dying, for planets also die. About her crept a ghost of atmosphere, the body eaten full away by iron rust and belching smoke until the plains, stretching wide, were sickly red, and no green showed from range to range and pole to pole.

Red as Mars.

Dead, or nearly so, with the broken tumble of her cities peopled with the lizard and the wind. And the spaceports, which had given birth to the empires of space, were charred and indistinct upon the breast of Mother Earth.

So thought Lars the Ranger sitting in the window of the Greater Council Hall, so he saw from this eminence above the world and the red plains.

He too was getting old. Strong and young he had voyaged far on dangerous ways to bring the treasure back, but now he voyaged no more. Science had prolonged the beating of his heart a thousand years beyond his time, but now he was old and stiff and the Council chamber was cold.

The voices were thin behind him. They echoed oddly in this reverberant tomb. Seats were here for all the Council members of full six hundred systems. But the seats were empty now and their metal threw back the reedy whine of the clerks who called them all to order, reading names which had been gone these seven hundred years, all formal, all precise, and noting that they were not here.

Mankin, Grand President of the Confederated Systems, sat hunched and aged upon his dais, looking out upon his servants, listening to the threadbare rite.

"Capella!"

Silence.

"Rigel Centaurus!"

Silence.

"Deneb and Kizar and Betelgeuse!"

Silence.

And onward for six hundred names.

Silence.

For they were mighty there in the stars and Mother Earth was old. They were thriving across a mighty span of ten thousand light-years. And Mother Earth had no longer any fuel. They had taken the oil from her deepest springs and the coal from her lowest mines. They had breathed her air and forged her steel and taken their argosies away. And behind them they had scant memory.

Earth had no power of money now, no goods, no trades, no fleet. And the finest of her strong young men had gone this long, long while. The lame, the halt, these and the dimmest of sight had stayed. And now there was nothing.

"Markab!"

"Achernar!"

"Polaris!"

No one there. No one there. No one there. No one.

Lars the Ranger stood and stiffly shook out his cloak. He

couched the ceremonial space helmet in his crookt arm and advanced formally to the dais. He bowed.

He might have reported there in the ritual that the fleets were ready and the armies strong, that as General of Space he could assure them all of the peace in space.

But he was suddenly conscious of who they were and how things stood and he said nothing.

There was Greto, once a wizard of skilled finance, sitting chin on breast in an advisor's chair. There was Smit, the valiant warrior of five hundred years ago. There was Mankin, tiny in his robe, crushed down by years and grief.

About Lars swirled, for an instant, the laughing staff of centuries back—young men with the giddy wine of high risk in their hearts. About Lars thundered the governing mandates of Earth to Space, to System Empires everywhere.

And then he saw the four of them and the clerks, alone here on a world which was nearly dead.

He broke ritual softly.

"There are no fleets and the armies have melted away. There is no fuel to burn in the homes, much less in the cannon. There is no food, there are no guns. I can no longer consider myself or this Council master of space and all that it contains."

They had all come there with a vague hope that it would break. And it had broken. And Greto came to his feet, his wasted body mighty and imposing still.

There was silence for a while and then Greto turned to the dais. "I can report the same. For fifteen long years I could have said nearly as much. But I admit this now. Earth is no more."

Smit lumbered upright. He scowled and clenched a black fist as he looked at Lars. "We have our fleets and our guns. Who has been here these last decades to know that they are without fodder? Bah! This thing can be solved!"

Mankin hunched lower, opened a drawer and brought out a tablet which he took. As he set down his water glass, he belched politely and looked from one to the next, bewildered, a little afraid. He had been able to handle many things in his day.

He fumbled with his reports and they were all the same. People were old and children were few. The food was gone and winter would be cold.

He cleared his throat. Hopefully he looked at Smit. "I was about to suggest that some measure be taken to remove the few thousands remaining here to some planet where food and fuel are not so dear. But I only hope that I can be advised—"

"You could remove nothing," said Greto, thrusting his hands into his pockets. "You could take nothing away. For there's not fuel to lift more than twenty ships from the surface of Earth. The cause may be lost, but I am not lost. Earth is no longer tenable as she is. I propose that, with credits long past due, I force the purchase of atmosphere manufacturing equipment and other needful things."

"Credits!" said Smit. "What do I know of credits? If this thing is at last in the light and the need is desperate, I can give them the promise of guns in their guts. Need they know?"

Mankin looked from one to the other. He was heartened a little, for he had begun to see these fabulous men as little more than companions of his desultory chess games. But he did not heed them too much.

He turned to Lars.

"What says the General of Armies and Admiral of Fleets?"

Lars the Ranger laid his helmet on the clerk's table. All semblance of formality fell from him as he took a pipe from his pocket, loaded it and lighted it with his finger ring. He looked from Mankin to Greto.

"My fleet," he said, "has not fired a jet in so many years that I have quite forgotten how many emergency charges were left aboard. I do know that mechanics and even officers have long since used all reserve atomic fuel for the benefit of lighting plants in the cities and our few remaining factories. At the most, on all our five continents I seriously doubt whether or not we retain enough fuel for more than two or three hundred light-years. That is, of course, for one of our minor destroyers. Hardly enough for an extended cruise of space.

"At the old Navy yard at the Chicago spaceport I daresay there may be four destroyers in more or less workable condition. Certainly there are enough spare parts in the battleships to complete them and make them usable. In our service lists we have a handful of technicians who, though they may be old, still retain some of their touch.

"We could probably beg enough food in the way of voluntary contributions to provision the trip. Perhaps we are just dreaming. We may be at best only old men sitting in the sun and thinking thoughts much better carried out by young sinews. But I for one would like to try.

"Today I walked through the streets of this city and an illusion gripped me. Once more I was a young man returning from a colonization in the Capella system. The sidewalks were lined with people, the unbroken pavement glittered before me thick with roses. Young boys and girls darted in and out amongst the crowd adding their shrill cries. I knew how great, how strong, Earth was. And then, the illusion faded and the pavement was broken and the roses were thorny weeds, and an old woman whined for bread at the street corner. I saw but one child in half a hundred blocks of walking, and he was ill.

"An old man is old and has nothing but memory. It is youth which plans, endeavors and succeeds. Frankly, gentlemen, I have but little hope. But I cannot stay, while even a few years remain, and know that Mother Earth which I served for all my thousand years is dying here, forgotten and unmourned."

He sat looking at them in a little while, puffing his pipe, swinging an ancient but well-polished boot, not seeing them but remembering.

Smit blustered to his feet. "We are speaking of dreams. I know very little of dreams but I demand to be told why our friend desires to beg for food? Are we still not the government? Must we dig in garbage cans to provision our government's expeditions and crawl in dung heaps for a few crumbs of combustium? The first right of any government is to enforce its will upon the people.

"I highly approve of the expedition. I demand that I be allowed to take one section of it. And I desire, if this matter be agreed upon, that all necessary writs and manifestos be placed in my hands to create it a reality."

Mankin looked nervous, took another tablet and washed it down. It had been three hundred years since an expedition of any major import had been planned in this chamber. All the major expeditions formed on Centauri now where food, fuel, and crews were plentiful. The bombastic tone of Smit had battered Mankin. He looked at Greto.

Greto was aware of the eyes upon him. He shifted his feet nervously. Hesitantly he said, "I approve of this expedition even though I have little hope of its success, for it will be very difficult to attend to the financing here. Our funds are in an impossible condition. Our currency is worthless. I take it that at least two units, perhaps four, will be sent. I myself would like the command of a unit. But how we are to finance the voyageurs is a problem I cannot readily solve. One Earth dollar can be valued no higher than one-thousandth of a cent on Capella. This means I must assemble millions." He rubbed his thumb against his forefinger. "They like money out there in those systems."

"Print it," said Smit. "Who'll know the difference? And if you are to command one of the units, then my advice is to print a lot of it."

Mankin coughed, he looked at the three of them and knew that it was he who must make the decision. A small flame of hope was leaping up in him now. He thrilled to the thought that Earth might once more prosper and send forth and receive commerce and trade. The strangely renewed vitality in Smit's voice gave him assurance.

"Gentlemen," he said, "you give me courage. Unless one of you has some objection to offer, I hereby decree that, if possible, three units be dispatched singly on this mission. They will progress as far as possible through the empires of space and the outer worlds and will return with whatever succor or tidings each has been able to obtain. This mission would be worthwhile even if you return with no more than a few hundred pounds of Element One Hundred and Seventy-Six. There must be some way, gentlemen, there *must* be some way."

Lars the Ranger stood up. "I shall order the preparation of three destroyer units and do what I can to provide them with fuel and food. If it is your will, I shall command one of them and place two at the disposition of Smit and Greto."

He about-faced and approached the door, where he turned. "I can hardly believe, gentlemen, that we have at last decided upon a course of vigorous action. Who knows but what we shall succeed?" The door of the Grand Council Chamber shut behind him.

Rumors spread far and wide across the planet and hope attended by many doubts turned people's eyes to the night skies where the stars blinked strong and young. A few broadcasting systems expended hoarded ergs of power to announce the departures of the expedition. Several old-time glass-paper editions of the newspapers in Greater Europa were given over exclusively to accounts of the various explorers. Smit was cited as the commander most likely to succeed, and his boasts at the spaceport before he took off were quoted as the purest truth.

A week after Smit's departure much space and talk was devoted to the fabulous Greto whose reputation as a financier had been founded fifteen hundred years ago with the Capella exploitation. They neglected the fact that it had been his further speculations which had impoverished him. They placed their hopes in his ability to "flimflam the money moguls of the greater empires."

When it came the time of Lars the Ranger to depart most of the news value of the expeditions was gone. Lars the Ranger had very little to say at the port. No one questioned the mechanics or remarked the fact that he had prudently taken weeks to groom his ship and to choose his crew. But old officers came and offered this one a map, that one a chart, and another a handful of bullets. And men who had ranged far and knew were on hand to bid him Godspeed and good luck amongst the spinning suns, the comets and dying stars. They toasted him in farewell and Lars the Ranger was gone.

Earth, only half remembering, waited and starved. Winter came. Frugal of their power, the expedition ships transmitted no messages. And Mankin, day after day moving thin-worn chessmen idly about on his board, bided his time.

The plains and mountains lay red, the thin air moaned bitterly cold about the towers of the government building. Sand drifted across the char-marks on the rocket field. Then spring came, and summer came, and were gone again, and another winter lay coldly dusty upon Earth's breast.

And one bitter morning a battered and rusty *Mercy,* which had borne Greto, came to rest on the government field. The instant it was sighted each man thought of his rank and vied at the doors of the Council chambers to give welcome to Greto. But it was no smooth and wily treasurer who came up to the big black doors. Greto hobbled, tired and bent, his space clothing ragged and out of repair. He was worn by hunger and all the bitter hardship of space. He did not need to push through the crowd, his appearance alone was enough to compel it back.

The doors opened before him and he entered. Mankin was about to mount the dais in formality when he saw Greto.

He stopped. Tears of sympathy leaped into his eyes. He came forward, arms outstretched. "Oh, my friend, my old friend," and he quickly seated him in a chair and brought him wine.

"Where are your officers and crew?" said Mankin. Greto did not need to answer. His eyes remained steadily on the floor. He turned over one hand and let it drop.

"From hunger when we had no food, and from sickness for which we had no medicine. I am ashamed, Mankin. I am ashamed to be here."

Mankin sat on a small stool and folded his hands in his lap. "I am sure you did what you could, Greto. Nothing can tell you how sorry I am. Perhaps things do not go so well with them."

Greto shook with sudden anger. He lifted his worn, starved face. His eyes glared up through the ceiling and at the unseen stars.

"Things go well enough up there. They are fat, they are wealthy." He grasped Mankin's hand. "They hate us. They hate us for the rules and mandates we put upon them. They hate us for the taxes that once we levied. They hate us for the wars we fought to stop. They hate us for the centuries we depreciated their currency to uphold the value of our own.

Pluteron in the Alpha Draco Empire laughed at me when I came. He laughed with hysteria and was still laughing when I left. There was no mirth in that laughter. There was only satisfaction. They hate us, Mankin. We shall get nothing from them, nothing!

"Cythara of Betelgeuse took a collection amongst the officers of his court to put a wreath in orbit about our sun after we were gone. I have been driven by laughter, by scorn."

He sat for a little while, chin on his breast. "Help me to my house, Mankin. I am afraid I have not long to live."

But it was Smit's return which spread the blackness of gloom across the world. For Smit was neither starved nor weary. Hate stood like a black aura around him through which cracked the lightning of his voice. Feet planted wide apart, he stood in the spaceport. He met all who came to him with such a tirade concerning the ungratefulness of the children in space that the world was shocked into hopeless rage.

He had gone the length of space, stopping everywhere he deemed it expedient. Everywhere he went he had met violence and suspicion. He had crossed the trail of Greto several times. He spoke of the Greto Plan to stabilize the currency of all space, with Earth as the central banking house, and the brutality with which the scheme, quite feasible, had been everywhere rejected. He told how Greto had sought to borrow a sufficient amount to rehabilitate Earth, and the outrageous interest that had been promised and how the governments which Greto had approached had fought Smit with the plan on his arrival.

But this was not the seat of bitterness with Smit. He told

them of space fleets equipped with weapons more deadly than those that Earth had ever known. One governor had given him a slingshot and had ordered him to fight a soldier equipped with a magnetic snare. And Smit had spent two weeks in a foul prison for driving in the governor's teeth.

He had been refused food, fuel, water, and medical attention for his men. He had been scorned and spat upon and mobbed from Centauri to Unuk. He had been insulted, rejected, scorned and given messages of such insulting import for Earth that here, delivering them, he seemed about to burst apart with rage.

The story of his return journey was one of violence. He had brought back his men but in the progress of returning need of fuel had forced him to loot the government arsenal at Kalrak. He had left the city burning behind him. Smit preached war, he preached it to old men, to rusted and broken machines, to tumbled and moss-grown walls.

Mankin opened the government radio for him and for four days Smit vainly attempted to recruit technicians and scientists to reconstruct the weapons that would be necessary to fight. Immediately after a broadcast in which he had attempted to stir up interest in an ancient and long-unused idea of germ warfare, an old officer of the republic's fleet barred his way as he attempted to leave the broadcasting building.

Smit, still affecting the dress he had worn on his return, filthy and ragged and seared as it might be, was offended at the clean, well-mended gray uniform.

"If you would help me, what are you doing here?" said Smit.

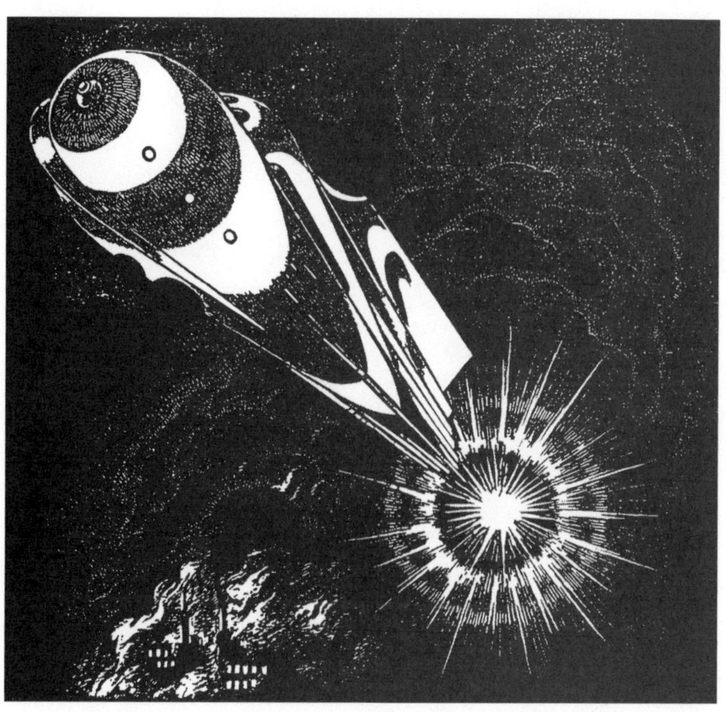

He had brought back his men but in the progress of returning need of fuel had forced him to loot the government arsenal at Kalrak. He had left the city burning behind him.

"I have ordered all men to repair to the military arsenal if they wish to forward this campaign."

The old officer smiled, undaunted by the blunt rage of Smit. "General," he said, "I have no ideas and I doubt that you would listen to any from me, but I was at the arsenal this morning and I do not think that we could do anything without fuel, weapons or the materials with which to make them. But I do not come here to advise you to abandon your idea. It will fail of its own accord. I came to ask you news of Lars the Ranger. Certainly if you found Greto's track, you must have news of Lars."

Mankin and several others were coming up the steps and Smit grasped at them as an audience.

"Yes, I have news of Lars. He had been in three places before I had arrived; he had said nothing, he had done nothing."

The old officer looked incredulous. "General, I am not of your branch of service and I would not argue with you, but I believe you play carelessly with the reputation of one who, if he commanded it could have audience wherever he went."

Smit was stunned. "Yes, certainly, audiences he did have. But he was given nothing. This I know."

Mankin was interested. "Did you learn nothing of him?" he asked Smit.

"All I know is that when I received audience after him I was heard coldly. My requests were refused, my demands were laughed at, and I was personally insulted. I know but little of this, but I can tell you this certainly, that you can expect nothing of Lars the Ranger."

The old officer turned away and, as he went down the steps, was seen to be laughing to himself.

For more than two months the campaign of Smit's raged feebly across the worn, arid surface of Earth. Where he had recruited, no army stood; where he had built, only junk could be seen. The waning efforts of technicians and bacteriologists finally stopped. Earth fell once more into an apathy, and at night men no longer looked hopefully at the stars.

In the first days of spring a mutter of reports came from the spaceport, and people wandered toward it in surprise to find a destroyer there, polished hull carefully repaired and a crew "at quarters" while the commander disembarked. An officer rushed from the crowd and grasped the hand of the voyager.

"Lars," he cried. And at the shout, several men in the crowd ran across the field to form a group around the newcomer. But the greatest number turned away. Two expeditions had arrived and the dream was spent, the hope was gone.

"What news?" said the old officer. Lars shrugged tiredly, he had aged on his voyage. "Little enough, my friend. They are vastly busy with their own concerns out there, but here I have brought at least some packets of food." And the quartermaster behind him signaled that the presents be brought down. When they were distributed, Lars walked toward the city.

Mankin heard of his arrival but did not go forth to meet him, for two disappointments were all that he could possibly bear. He had been sitting in the chill of the Council room when he received the tidings from his clerk. He just nodded hopelessly.

Lars entered the chamber and stood for a little while, feeling the coldness of it, looking at the withered Mankin in his chair. Lars came forward and put his helmet down upon the table.

Mankin spoke, "You have been gone for a long while, Lars."

"What of Greto and Smit?"

"They have both returned. Greto, I am afraid, is dying. He is sick rather with insults than with disease. Smit for some time was a man deprived of reason and he wanders now about the countryside speaking to no one, eating only what is thrust into his hand. He is a beaten man, Lars. This expedition was ill-starred. It would have been better that we had died at least with our dignity rather than to beg for crusts and make fools laugh. As the iron has eaten our air, so has this expedition drained the last sparks of vitality from the two who went before you. It was ill-starred, Lars."

Lars was about to speak, but Mankin again held up his hand.

"No, do not tell me. You have brought back your men, you have brought back your ship. Perhaps you have begged a little fuel, perhaps you have a little food. But you have nothing with which to save Earth. This I know."

Lars shook his head slowly. "You are right, Mankin. I have brought nothing. I did not expect to receive anything, since I did not beg. I did not threaten. In some places I heard of Greto's schemes. They hated him because they hated the financial control which Earth in her power exercised over the outer empires. In all the immensity of space there is not a man who would give a plugged mean coin to save a single child on Earth, if it meant the restoring of the financial tyranny which once we exercised."

"I know this," said Mankin sadly. "We hoped for too much."

Lars again shook his head. "No, Mankin, we were greedy for too much. Perhaps I have failed, perhaps I have not failed. I do not know."

"What did you tell them?" asked Mankin, not wanting hope to rise in his heart. "What did you tell them that you dare believe they might help us?"

"I did not tell them very much. And I thought first of how I might gain their goodwill. I found immediately that it could not be purchased or begged. I am afraid, Mankin, that I have amused myself at your expense."

This shocked the ancient president. He leaped to his feet. "You had better explain that, Lars!"

"I dined with them," said Lars. "I looked at their fleets, I admired their dancing girls, I saw their crops, and had the old battle places pointed out to me. And I told them stories. And this, reminding them, stimulated many tales. I asked for nothing, Mankin. I did not expect anything. I hope for nothing now. I am sorry that this is the report I must render."

"You had better go," said Mankin quietly.

For a month Lars, nearly ostracized, lived at the Navy yard in the improved destroyer, receiving old shipmates, giving presents from his frugal stock but going unaddressed in the streets. He heard nothing but condemnation for "the man who did not even try."

And then, one morning the town was shaken by a terrible

roar and with certainty that vengeance had been their return for the expedition, the populace tumbled from their beds to find six great gleaming spheres on the spaceport landing. They were larger than any other space vehicle these people on Earth had ever seen. From them came tumbling young men, well fed and laughing. Then they began to unload equipment.

No one dared to address the newcomers. With a hysterical certainty that they were about to be enslaved, the people of the capital, taking what little food they had, began to stream out of the far gate. A radio message from Asia was broadcast to the effect that fourteen huge vessels, unidentified, were landing troops. Greater Europa reported being besieged but said that no overt act had been made and all was being done to evacuate the population before bombardment.

Mankin received the reports in terror on his dais. He called together his cabinet. Noteworthily omitting Lars, he spent some fruitless six hours in feeble and frightened debate on measures of defense. No one came to him from the enemy forces and he felt, at last, that he must surrender before lives were lost.

When he and his staff went forward from the palace, they found that nineteen new vessels lay in the plain beyond the city. And that an encampment was being hastily constructed.

He was met by four boisterous young officers, each one from a different empire, all in working dress. The first of them, caught by the dignity of the cabinet and the president, and recognizing them as people of authority, quickly turned to his friends and sent one of them racing back toward a nearby sphere.

Mankin took a grip on his courage, he had never looked for the day when he would have to surrender Earth to an attacking force. But now that he saw that it could not be helped, he could only try to carry it forth with dignity.

He was somewhat amazed at the courteous mien of the young officers, who did not speak to him but respectfully waited for a sign from the large spaceship.

In a moment or two, hastily pulling on a uniform coat and adjusting his epaulettes, a large middle-aged man strode toward the group. He stopped at a distance of five paces from Mankin, identified the chest ribbon and the ancient robe of office and then spoke.

"You are President Mankin?" he said politely.

Mankin stiffened himself and answered. "Yes. Whom have I the pleasure of addressing?"

"I am General Collingsby," he said. With a crisp military bow, he extended his hand. "It is an honor to meet you, sir," said Collingsby, "I am sorry I occasioned you the difficulty of having to come to the port. I am ashamed at my own discourtesy in not having called on you immediately. However, command has its responsibilities and, as these are supply forces, there has been considerable trouble in establishing consignments and in distributing our various fleets over the surface of the earth."

He coughed. "Excuse me, sir, but by Jupiter, your air is certainly thin here! My blood pressure must be up off the meter. But here, permit me to invite you into my cabin where it is more comfortable, and we can talk at leisure."

Mankin straightened his shoulders. "Sir, I thank you

for your courtesy. I can only say that I hope that you will observe the various usages of war and that you will treat your prisoners without inhumanity and that you will occasion as little suffering as possible."

General Collingsby looked startled and then embarrassed. It was easily read upon his face that he had no clue to the meaning of Mankin's statements.

"My dear sir," he stammered, "I do not understand you. Has not my own governor, Voxperius, contacted you concerning our arrival?"

"General," said Mankin, "the ionized beams of communication between Earth and her former colonies have been severed for more than seventy years. I am afraid we have not had sufficient power or even need to continue them in operation."

Collingsby looked at his staff in round-eyed wonder and then at Mankin. He looked beyond the group before him and his face lighted. "Perhaps this gentleman can clarify matters."

Mankin turned to see Lars the Ranger, with a small group of officers, approaching.

Collingsby eagerly grabbed Lars by the arm. "My dear fellow, would you please acquaint your president with the true complection of affairs. By Jupiter, I had not thought of it before but it certainly does look like an invasion. Oh, I am ashamed of this, Lars! I am ashamed of it! What a panic we must have caused. But I was certain that my government and the other governments had contacted Earth. Didn't you know, Lars?"

Mankin was bewildered. For the first time he had a clear look at what was poured into the encampment. He saw huge machines being unloaded. He saw that they were already at work with some of them. Beams were playing across the plains and at each place one struck, puffs of smoke rose. Others were drilling into the earth and sending up high plumes of exhaust. Mankin suddenly realized that they must be reoxygenators replacing humus, injecting heat under the crust. A faintness came over him. He could not believe what he saw and he could not hope.

Lars turned to him. "I could not tell you, I could not promise you. But truly, I did nothing."

Collingsby interrupted with a sharp, "No, he did nothing. He came and sang us old ballads and told us the hero tales of Earth; he reminded us of the heritage we had behind us; and of what we owed the mother planet. She was drained of her blood for our sakes. He made us see the quiet ocean and the green hills where our fathers lived. And then, having shrugged and said it was no more, he moved on.

"He went all through space and told his tales. In the empires everywhere school children formed subscriptions, governments formed expeditions, scientists worked, on what had to be done—but here, certainly, President Mankin, you can see how this would be. After all, Earth is the 'Mother' of all the stars. And somewhere in the heart of every man in the empires lurks a fondness for the birthplace of his race. For our histories are full of Earth and all our stories, all our great triumphs, contain the name of Earth. Should we then let her die?

"And so we have come here, these combined forces, to make the old land green again, to replace the oceans, to rebuild an atmosphere, to make the rivers run, to put fish in the streams, and game in the hills.

"We'll make this place a shrine, complete and vital as once it was, where Inter-Empire councils may arbitrate the disputes of space. Here we can meet on the common ground of birth and, in the halo of her greatness, find the answers to our problems. For in the long run the problems and the answers change very little. All the fundamental questions have been asked and solved on Earth before; and they will be again.

"But come," said Collingsby. "We have less than a week to repair all. It is," he asked Lars, "just a week to July fourth, is it not? And that was the anniversary of the launching of the first expedition to Earth's moon, wasn't it?"

"But come into my ship where we can have some refreshments. There will be time enough to stand around in the sun when all these fields are green."

They looked at Lars and he smiled at them. Mankin swallowed back a lump of emotion in his throat.

"Lars, why didn't you tell me you had saved Earth with a song?"

Tough Old Man

CHAPTER ONE

Tractor Takeoff

THE young officer named George Moffat was inspired, natty and brilliant that day he stepped down from the tramp spacecan to the desolate plains of Ooglach. Fresh from the Training Center of the Frontier Patrol in Chicago, on Earth, newly commissioned a constable in the service, the universe was definitely the exclusive property of Mr. Moffat.

With the orders and admonitions of his senior captain—eighteen light-years away—George Moffat confronted the task with joy. Nothing could depress him—not even the shoddy log buildings which made up Meteorville, his home for the next two years—if he lasted.

But he'd last. Constable Moffat was as certain of that as he was of his own name. He'd last!

"This is a training assignment," he had been told by the senior captain. "For the next two years you will work with Old Keno Martin, the senior constable in the service. When you've learned the hard way you can either replace him as the senior constable or have a good assignment of your own. It all depends on you.

"You'll find Old Keno a pretty hard man to match. I've never met him myself. He came to us as an inheritance from Ooglach when we took it over—he'd been their peace officer for fifteen years and we sent him a commission sight unseen. He's been a constable for twenty years and he's pretty set in his ways, I guess."

Moffat had known very well what he was being told. The Frontier Patrol always sent a man to the God-forgotten ends of nowhere under instruction for his first two years of service. The harder the assignment, the greater the compliment to the recruit. That he had drawn "Old Keno" Martin was compliment beyond the highest adulation.

"Good Lord!" his running mate Druid had told him. "Old Keno is more of a legend than a man. You know what's happened to the only three recruits sent to him for training? He wore them out and did them in. Every one of them came back and turned in his resignation. George, I wish you luck. By golly, you'll need it!"

Constable Moffat, stepping through the frozen mud of the main street of Meteorville, wasn't daunted even now. The multicolored icy wastes, the obvious savageness and antagonism of the inhabitants who glowered at him as he passed in his horizon blue and gold, the sagging temperature that registered thirty below at high noon, neither could these daunt him.

Resigned, did they? Well, he was George Moffat and no old, broken-down, untrained ex-peace-officer-made-constable was going to show him up. Old Keno was going to be retired when they found a replacement for him. George Moffat, strong and young, full of morale and training, already considered Old Keno as good as replaced.

He gloried in the obvious fact that the patrol was hated here. Ooglach, furthest outpost of Earth's commerce, held more than its share of escaped criminals. The men who watched him from windows and walks would meet his cool gaze. He became more and more conscious of what he was and where he was until the problem of Old Keno dwindled to nothing.

A man had to be hard in the patrol. The instructors at school were fond of saying that. He had to be able to endure until endurance seemed his ordinary lot in life. He had to be able to shoot faster and more accurately than any human could be expected to shoot and he had to be able to thrive under conditions which would kill an unconditioned man. George Moffat could do all these things. Question was, at his age could Old Keno?

Constable George Moffat entered the low building which boasted the battered sign: *Frontier Constabulary, Ooglach.* He entered and at first glance felt pity for the man he was to relieve.

Old Keno Martin, in a patched blue uniform shirt, sat at a rough plank desk. He was scribbling painfully with a pen which kept tripping in the rough official paper and scattering small blots. It was aching cold in the room and the ashes of the fireplace were dead.

He was a spare man of uncertain age, George observed, and he had no more idea of how to keep and wear a uniform than he probably had about grand opera. A battered gray hat sat over his eyes, two blasters were belted about his waist, both on one side, one lower than the other.

The squadroom was bare, without ornament or comforts, the only wall decoration being a mildewed copy of the Constitution of the United States. Some cartridge boxes and several rifles lay upon a shelf, some report books on the desk.

This, observed Moffat with a slightly curled lip, was law and order on Ooglach!

Old Keno looked up. He saw the horizon blue and gold and stood.

"I," said Moffat, "have just been ordered up from base." He handed his sheaf of official papers and identification over and Old Keno took them and scanned them with disinterest.

To George it seemed that his attitude clearly said, "Here's another one of them to be broken and sent on his way. A boot kid, badly trained and conceited in the bargain." But then, thinking again, George wasn't sure that that was Old Keno's attitude. The man, he knew suddenly, was going to be very hard to predict.

Old Keno offered his hand and then a chair. "I'm Keno Martin. I'll have the boy stir up the fire for you if you're cold. Newcomers find it chilly here in Meteorville."

Old Keno returned to his reports while George Moffat, seeing no sign of the boy mentioned, glanced yearningly at the dead fireplace. Suddenly George realized what he was doing. The lot of a constable was endurance. If Old Keno, knowing he was coming, had already started the program of hazing, George was ready. Grimly he refused the warmth for himself and concentrated on Old Keno.

"I understand," said Keno after a while, "that if you measure up I'm to be retired from service."

"Well—" began George.

"Wouldn't know what to do with myself," said Old Keno decidedly. "But that's no bar to your measuring up. If you can you can and that's all there is to it. *I* won't stand in your way."

Young George said to himself that he doubted it. The temperature must be twenty below in this room. Inside his gloves his hands felt blue and frostbitten. "I'll bet you won't," George told himself.

"Matter of fact," said Old Keno, "I'm kind of glad you're here. The general run of crime is always fairly heavy and this morning it got heavier. It will be good to have help on this job. I've been kind of hoping they'd send me an assistant—"

"I'll bet you have," said George to himself.

"—that could really take it, of course," continued Old Keno. "Ooglach is a funny place. Hot as the devil in some places, cold in others. Requires versatility. You know why this place is important?"

"Well, I—"

"This planet is a meteor deposit. About fifteen or twenty million meteors a day fall into its atmosphere, but that isn't a patch on what it used to get before the atmosphere formed as it is. Its face is studded with the things and there are holes all over the place.

"We ship several hundred billion dollars' worth of industrial diamonds from here every year. Naturally we have to mine the bulk of them out of old meteors and that keeps a miner population around—which is always a tough one. Some of those stones are gemstones. They're a United States monopoly and it's our job to see that they don't get lifted. We frown on all illegal export—especially when it begins with murder."

Moffat perked up. He forgot about the cold room. This was what he had been training for. He was very conscious of his superiority in such cases. The latest methods of crime detection had been built into him as second nature. His young body had been trained to accomplish the most strenuous manhunts. Mentally he was well balanced, physically he was at his peak. He knew it and he was anxious to prove it.

"You've got some idea of who is doing this?" said Moffat.

"Well, shouldn't be too hard. Of course, there's plenty of tough gents on Ooglach who wouldn't stop at anything—but the point is they're cowed. My angle is, the people who did this must be new. They murdered a mine guard up at Crater 743 and emptied the safe of a month's haul. That would be about thirty-five million dollars in gems.

"Any man who had been around here any time would have known better. That means the gents who did it probably came in their own spaceship. It's probably parked beyond the radar detection sphere—somewhere to the south. No, it wasn't local talent."

Moffat almost smiled. Old Keno's faith in himself seemed monstrous to him. He looked with interest at the old constable and realized with a start that all his own studies in criminology and physiognomy had not fitted him to make an accurate estimate of Keno Martin's true character. The man was elusive.

"So, if it's all the same to you," said Keno, "we'll just put together a kit and take out of here for the mine. I just got this report half an hour ago and I stopped here long enough to write this dispatch for my boy to take to that spacecan you came in. I want this data relayed to other planets, though of course we'll probably get these people a long time before they get away. You all ready to go?"

He looked with interest at the old constable and realized with a start that all his own studies in criminology and physiognomy had not fitted him to make an accurate estimate of Keno Martin's true character.

For a moment Moffat was dismayed. He had considered himself fit and ready and yet he knew that his long trip on the tramp had wearied him enormously. You don't sleep and eat well on a tramp and how welcome would be a few hours of rest! But he banished all thought of it. Keno would know he was tired. This was just another way of wearing him down.

"I'm ready," he said. "Just tell your boy to bring my case from the ship. I feel fine."

"Good," said Old Keno. He opened the back door and yelled in some remarkable gibberish at the shed. Then he took down from a shelf several boxes of cartridges, looked to the loads in his guns and handed a rifle to Moffat.

Old Keno waited patiently at the door until a slab-faced native brought a high-speed tractor around front and then, after placing the cartridges in the cab, Old Keno mounted up.

"Wait a minute," said Moffat. "I don't see any food. How long are we going to be gone?"

The old constable looked embarrassed. "I'm sorry about that. My mind was just so busy with other things. Bring out a case of rations from the kitchen."

Moffat smiled to himself. This campaign was so obvious. He brought the rations and threw them into the back of the cab and then, eyes on the old constable, mounted up in his turn.

Suddenly he was assailed with a doubt. Maybe it was just senility that had made Old Keno forget. A man wouldn't go tearing off into any trackless waste without food just to show up a new recruit. Hmm . . . maybe headquarters had its reasons for wanting to replace this man.

"Where's your coat?" said Moffat, eyeing the patched sleeves of Old Keno's uniform shirt.

"That's so," said the old constable, looking oddly at Moffat. "I forgot that too, I guess." He bawled at the boy, who brought up a heavy service mackinaw. But Old Keno did not put it on. He laid it across the back of the seat and addressed himself to the controls.

The revving motor sent great plumes of white snow spiraling upwards. Several curious folks came into the street to look. Moffat glanced at the old constable and felt a genuine wave of pity. "Poor Old Keno," he thought.

The yellow sky lay hard against the blinding plain. In the far distance a range of hundred-thousand-foot peaks reached forever skyward, white and orange in their perpetual covering of frost. The tractor sped across the wastes at two hundred miles per hour, skimming the hummocks, its hydraulic seats riding easy while the treads bucked, spun and roared. A high fog of snow particles was left behind them and the cold which had been intense at the beginning began to turn Moffat's blood to ice crystals in his veins.

At last he surrendered. "Isn't there a heater in this thing?" he said.

CHAPTER TWO

Rugged Going

OLD Keno flushed. "I'm sorry. I've got so much on my mind I didn't even think of it." And he reached down to throw a button on the panel, which brought an immediate trickle of faintly warm air into the cab, raising the interior temperature from a minus fifty to a mere minus twenty.

Moffat tried not to show how eagerly he received this succor from his distress. He was beginning to feel a little frightened of Old Keno. There he sat in his shirt sleeves, oblivious of weather. Beside him was Moffat, bundled to the eyes in all that the service could offer a man in the way of warmth—all of which was not enough.

By golly, thought Moffat, a man could pretty well perish riding in one of these things if he wasn't careful. He glanced sideways at Keno. The old constable did not find anything unusual about his uncoated state.

"He's senile," Moffat decided. "He's unable to feel anything." And then again he thought, "He's trying to run me out. I'll stick it if it's the last thing I ever do on Ooglach." And he knew with a slight shudder that this very well *might* be the last thing he did on Ooglach or anywhere else!

Half an hour later they pulled up beside the shaft of Crater 743, where the mine buildings clustered under a ten-foot coating of snow and ice. Their presence had been seen from afar and a small knot of men awaited them. Their greeting was respectful, bordering on awe.

"I've been watching for you, Constable," said the foreman. "I'm very sorry to have to trouble you but—"

"I suppose you trampled up all the clues," said Keno gruffly.

The crowd parted to let him through. They had known better than to touch the murdered man or the safe or to walk on tracks, and Keno and Moffat were able to inspect the scene as it had been found at dawn by the cook.

Keno looked at the dead man and muttered to himself, "Forty-five Mauser at the range of two feet. Silencer employed. Asleep when he was hit. Alarm signal shorted out by the intruder. Safe opened with an alpha torch."

He knelt before the broken door and Moffat was amazed to hear him muttering the code of arches and whorls which would identify future fingerprints.

Moffat, puzzled, got down beside the old constable and at length, by catching the light just right, was able to make out the fact that at least there was a fingerprint there. But even with all his training he knew he would need powder and a magnifier to read that mark.

He looked wonderingly at Keno. Either the old constable was pulling his leg or he actually could read that print. It could be a bluff. After all, what did a lone fingerprint matter in this case?

Moffat was additionally puzzled to find that the crew at the mine had been so meticulous as to avoid obliterating the tracks of the retreating felons. He was impressed against his wish by this. It meant these people really walked lightly where

Old Keno was concerned. He was wondering if Keno had remembered to bring a plaster cast outfit when he heard Keno grumbling.

"Leader's about five feet tall, walks with a bad limp, been in the Russian army, very quick, probably shoots left-handed. The other two men are ex-convicts, both with dark hair, heavy features—one about a hundred and ninety-five pounds, the other two hundred and thirty. They rely entirely on the leader for orders. They'll fight if told. Come along, Constable Moffat. We'll see what can be done to intercept these people."

Moffat could have deduced a number of these things, but not all of them. He was bemused by it. This old man was not bluffing! And that fact made Keno loom larger than before. Moffat began to dwindle in his own estimation.

Without a word to the waiting men Old Keno climbed into the cab, slammed the door, waited briefly for Moffat to get settled and went off at full speed along the clear track of a departing skimmer.

Young Constable Moffat was not prepared for the accuracy of this tracking. He was beginning to understand why the other young recruits had quit here and resigned from service. Old Keno was not only good, he was dismaying. A man's ego wouldn't long withstand the pummeling of such exhibitions of endurance and manhunter sense that Old Keno had displayed to him today.

Now the old man was following the thin line left by the skimmer—and he was following it at two hundred and fifty miles per hour.

As a skimmer is driven by a tractor propeller and rises on

stub wings to travel, it leaves only an occasional scratch in the snow. Yet Keno Martin was following this scratch. He was evidently seeing it some hundreds of yards ahead and turning accurately whenever it turned.

They raced across the trackless expanse, going south. They were silent for the most part. The dumbbell suns gradually sank until the shadows of the ice hummocks were long and blue across the wastes of crystal white.

Moffat was tired. The trip on the space-tramp had been a hard one, and the long hours of traveling over these blinding, glaring ice fields were just too much. It would have been too cold for the human endurance of any man who had not had months of conditioning to these temperatures. Moffat had had that conditioning. But each agonizing breath of frozen air came closer to breaking him.

Then he realized that Old Keno, wrestling the tractor, showed no signs of fatigue. Insensibly, Moffat's estimation of his own capabilities dropped. He began to regard Keno with a sort of awe.

"Don't you want me to take it for a while?" he said at last out of a guilty conscience.

"Sorry, this will get tough as soon as those suns set and we'll have to rely on our spots. I'll just hold on if it's all the same to you."

After a while young Moffat began to fidget. Then he suddenly realized what was the matter. "Say, aren't you hungry?" he said.

Old Keno looked at him blankly. Then he said, "Oh yes, yes, of course. Get yourself something to eat."

Moffat started to turn and in that moment realized all the sensations that a man must feel who is caught in a straitjacket. He could not swivel more than an inch in either direction. His heavy uniform coat was frozen solid upon him.

Impotently he cursed the supply station eighteen light-years away. The trickle of heat had melted a filter of snow from under the windshield. While it was still daylight it had dampened his coat. As the suns set, the temperature had dropped to about fifty below zero.

"Turn up the heat," he said plaintively. Old Keno blinked at him.

"That's all the heat there is," he apologized.

"Well, hit me with your fist or something," said Moffat. Old Keno blinked again. "It's my coat," said Moffat.

Keno grunted and brought a backhand slap against Moffat's chest which cracked the ice sheathing. With the disintegration begun, the young constable could move about. He procured a can of rations.

These had been packed by some far-off organization which never had expected for a minute that anyone was going to eat any of them. Theoretically, when one took off the lid heat was instantaneously generated through all the food. Moffat broke the cover and for the next ten seconds—but no more—the mass was warm. Before he could get the first mouthful between his teeth the savage cold had frozen it through.

He started to complain and then he looked at the stolid Keno. Frozen rations were nothing to the old man—he was munching mechanically on the food. "Well," thought Moffat, "if he can take it I can." And he reached into an inner pocket with his clumsy glove and brought out a chocolate bar, which flew into splinters each time he took a bite from it.

"You'd better let me drive," said Moffat. "You'll need some of your strength later on. We don't want to get tired out."

He intended this as a vengeful reference to Old Keno's age. But the senior constable paid no attention whatever.

"I said you'd better let me drive for a while," said young Moffat.

"You sure you can handle this thing?" said Old Keno.

"We were taught all types of vehicles in school," said Moffat a little savagely.

"Well," said Old Keno doubtfully, "I suppose we've got more time than we really need. And we've been making pretty good speed. You might as well start learning now as ever." He set the automatic control on the tractor and when it reached a level stretch, during which the control could operate, they swiftly switched.

Moffat may have been bitterly cold outside but he was burning within. So the old man thought they'd lose speed if he drove, did he? Well, since when did youth take any lessons from age on that subject?

The dark was very thick and the floodlights were piercingly bright on the track ahead. The multicolored cliffs and valley of ice fled past them. Moffat found that it was extremely difficult to accurately trace the track. More than once Old Keno had to tap him sharply to keep him from straying.

Each time Old Keno tapped, young Moffat seethed anew.

There sat the old fool in his patched blue shirt, not caring any more about this cold than he did about rations. Obviously the old man was out to show him up, to make a fool out of him, to break his spirit. Obviously Keno expected to send him back to headquarters with his resignation written and ready to be turned in. Well, that would never happen.

The tractor roared and whined. Young Moffat let it out to two hundred and ninety miles an hour. At this speed the ice hummocks were a blur and even more often now Old Keno had to tap him to keep him on the track.

"Pretty soon," said Old Keno, "we'll start down. The snow level at this time of the year stops at about twenty-three thousand feet. You'll find Ooglach's got a lot in the way of drops and rises. There isn't any sea level properly speaking.

"We've got three seas but from the lowest to the highest there's an eighteen-thousand-foot difference in elevation. I'd hate to think of what would happen if they ever got connected.

"It's two hundred and ninety thousand feet from the lowest point on this planet to the highest. Nature scraped her up some when she was built. I guess she wasn't rightly intended for men. This plateau we're on is the most comfortable spot you'll discover."

Moffat listened with some disbelief. The old man was just trying to scare him away.

"The low valleys are all scorchers," Keno continued, "and the one where I think our friends are hanging out will be running about a hundred and fifty degrees now that the sun has set."

Young Moffat glanced sideways at him. “Warm, huh?”

“Well, it isn’t so bad once you get used to it,” said Old Keno. “By the way, you’ll want to start looking sharp now. We’ll have to turn off these lights. If we show them as we come over the top edge into the valley they’ll have plenty of time to get away in their spacecan. D’ye mind?” he said.

CHAPTER THREE

WRECKED

YOUNG Moffat thought savagely that if Old Keno could drive in the dark, as he had immediately after sundown, *he* certainly could. He reached down and threw the light switch.

Instantly, as a reaction, the whole world was black to him. He lost his sense of direction utterly. He was lightblinded and yet hurtling forward over uneven terrain at tremendous speed. He did not know whether he was turning to right or left and felt certain that he was about to shoot on a tangent from his course. In a panic young Moffat grabbed at the light panel but he was too late.

He felt the tractor start to turn. He felt Old Keno's savage pull at the levers which might avert the disaster. Then there was a terrifying crash and a roar, a splintering of glass, the scream of a dismembered motor and the dying whine of treads running down to a slow clatter.

Young Moffat picked himself up off an ice hummock two hundred feet from the scene of the wreck. He was dazed and bleeding. One of his gloves was missing and one of his boots was ripped all the way down the side, exposing his flesh to the killing winds of the night. For a moment he could not tell ground from stars. A few planets of his own invention were spinning giddily in space.

After a bit he located the direction of the wreck by the

sound of dripping fuel. He crawled back to it fearfully. He thought perhaps Old Keno lay dead within it. Moffat saw his own track in the luminous snow and found that he had plowed straight through a feathery snowbank, which alone had saved him.

Two feet above or below the course he had taken would have brought him into disastrous collision with enormous lumps of ice.

He fumbled over the area and at last located the dark crushed blob of the wreck. All his resentment for Keno was gone now. He knew that this was his own fault. He felt that if the old man were dead he could never forgive himself. He should have known he would not be able to drive at that speed with the lights out.

"Where are you?" he shouted into the cab, fumbling through the torn upholstery.

With a sob he slid in through the broken windshield and felt along the upended floor for Old Keno's body. But it was not there.

Young Moffat scuttled crabwise out of the fuming wreckage and began to look through the debris for a pocket torch.

"Well, I'm mighty glad to find that you're all right, son."

Moffat leaped upright as though he'd been shot.

"I walked on down the line," said Old Keno. "We're within about two hundred yards of the edge there and we would have been starting down soon anyway. So we ain't lost much time."

Moffat threw the torch he had found to the ground before him. If Old Keno had only been reproving or solicitous—if he had shown something, anything, but the calm, cool detachment of a man who, immediately after a wreck, would walk on a little further just to see how things were . . .

"I might have been killed," said young Moffat.

"Oh no," said Old Keno. "On my way up to the rim I looked at you there in the snow and saw that you were all right."

The inferred superiority of this was almost more than Moffat could stand. He was rising to a point of fury.

"Well, you'd better not stand there," said Keno, the wind tugging at his thin shirt. "You're liable to get cold. Come along."

Moffat fumbled through the drift and found his glove. Then he turned to trudge after Keno. As he cooled he found that something terrible and devastating had happened to his ego.

He had always considered himself so competent. And he had always felt that older men were used up and worn out. Now he found that a man who must be well over sixty easily had the edge on him both in poise and in endurance. The cool rationality of the fellow had gnawed at young Moffat's ego until its borders were frayed.

Sunk now in his own estimation to the level of a schoolboy who is subject to tantrums, young Moffat followed in Keno's tracks and presently came up with the old man.

If he had expected an end to travail because they were to go downhill into a valley, Moffat was mistaken. One of Ooglach's moons, yellow and gibbous, had begun to rise. By its light, the enormous crater before them, thirty thousand feet deep, lay like the entrance to the infernal regions.

Its black sides were rough and jagged and precipitous.

At twenty-three thousand feet one could see, by looking across several miles to the other side, where the snow level ended. Below that clung a handful of trees, ghostly now in the brilliant moonlight.

Young Moffat stared at the precipice before him. There was a track down it which angled off at a steep grade, cut probably by some mining survey expedition. But Keno was not considering such a path.

"We've lost quite a lot of time," said Old Keno. "We'll have to make up for it one way or the other. Let's pitch off here and scramble on down the side wall. It's only about thirty thousand feet and the jumps are pretty easy.

"I've been here before. I didn't take this side but I don't expect we'll run into a lot of trouble. Now—you keep close to me and don't go losing your hold on anything and falling because we don't want to mess this up again tonight."

Young Moffat took the implied criticism haggardly. Old Keno slid forward over the ice and started to drop down from crevice to crevice with a swift agility which would have done credit to an orangutan.

Young Moffat started out eagerly enough but in a very few minutes he discovered how bruised and shaken he had been by the wreck. And Old Keno, who must have been just as bruised, was stretching out a lead on him which was in itself a blunt criticism.

Harassed and scrambling, young Moffat tried his best to keep up. He slid from one block of ice to the next, scraped his shins on pinnacles, cut his hands on ledges and, as the drop increased, time after time hung perilously to a crumbling chunk of basalt over eternity. He needed all his strength to get across each gap. And his foot hurt where his boot was torn.

Old Keno, far, far below and evidently having no trouble, constantly widened the gap. Young Moffat's lungs were aching. If he had been too cold before, he was too hot now. His uniform was shortly in ribbons and by the time he had gone down three thousand feet he gladly abandoned the jacket forever. He used only one sleeve of it to bind up a shin which really could have used a few stitches put in by a competent doctor.

He was getting weaker as the swings and leaps took more and more heavy toll of him. He began to look down and ahead through a reddish haze which each time told him that the gap was getting wider and that Old Keno was having no trouble.

An hour later he came up, an aching, half-sobbing wreck. He hit against a soft form. He could not even see the old man. He slumped down on a boulder.

"Well, I'm glad you caught up to me," said Old Keno. "Now let's get moving. I took a look down into the valley and I got the spacecan spotted down there. They got a little fire lighted. Don't drop so far behind again."

Young Moffat cleared his gaze and looked at Old Keno. "That man," thought Moffat, "is going to kill me yet."

After all this terribly arduous mountaineering through the dark, over crevasses and down pinnacles and chimneys, swinging by razor-sharp outcrops to crumbling ledges, Old

Keno Martin didn't even have the grace or politeness to be short of breath. In the moonlight he was still his neat, somewhat faded self.

Beaten through and through, his conception of himself so thoroughly shot that only a miracle performed by himself could ever bring it back to life, young Moffat did his best to follow.

Thirty thousand feet is a long way down! And the difficulties of the descent made it also a long way around. Time after time Old Keno waited for him. Never a word of encouragement, never a word of comment on the difficulties of the descent—Old Keno was neither short of breath nor apparently tired of limb.

Hours later, when they at last came to the bottom of that scorching hell, Moffat supposed that he had at least passed through the worst of it. His breath was sobbing in and out of him. His body was a rack of pain. The only thing that had kept him going this long was the knowledge that the worst was almost over. Certainly he had no more to experience. But he was wrong!

As Old Keno had said, it was a hundred and fifty degrees here in this crater. The sand was baking hot. He reached his hand up to his eyes and swept away some of the perspiration which was blinding him. His lips were thickened by dehydration.

The night was so hot and so dry that it pulled the moisture out of a man with a physical force, cracking his skin and drying his eyes until it was torture to keep them open longer than a minute at a time.

"Don't walk forward," said Keno. "There's a two-thousand-foot drop about twenty feet in front of us."

Moffat, stumbling forward, hadn't even realized he had caught up with Keno again. He was startled by the voice and he backed up a few steps. He concentrated his eyes on the spot Keno indicated and at last he saw the dark chasm. Gingerly he approached the edge.

He felt that he was looking into the very bowels of the planet although he could see nothing but blackness. He sensed the awesome depth of it. He stepped back cautiously, afraid that if he made a sudden movement he might fall headlong over the edge. The heat waves coming up from that black hole made him dizzy and his legs felt as though they might slip out from under him at any second. He turned back to Keno.

"We're within a quarter mile of them," said Old Keno. "I doubt if they got wind of us. It's a heck of a long ways back there to the ridge and they probably figured we was a meteorite like I thought they would. If they saw our crash at all, that is. That crew can't have been here more than ten or twenty minutes but they got a fire goin' already. Smell it?"

CHAPTER FOUR

Live Targets

MOFFAT sniffed at the wind in vain. He could not discover the least odor of wood smoke. Just breathing this air was enough to sear the lungs and burn scars on the throat without trying to smell anything in the bargain. He looked wonderingly at the old constable.

"They'll be boiling some fresh meat they got back at the mine," said Old Keno. "It wouldn't keep long down here and they probably haven't any galley in their spacecan. I figured I'd smell wood smoke when I got here, the second I noticed that a haunch of baysteer had been ripped from the drying racks outside the guard's shack at the mine."

Trained arduously, given the highest grades in detection, the young constable felt insensibly lessened again. He was failing every test. He had missed an important clue. Hurriedly he changed the subject. "How'd they cross this gap?" he asked.

"Oh, they're on this side of it all right," said Old Keno. "I saw their last tracks back there about a quarter of a mile. They turned off to the left and we're like to find them about a quarter of a mile up the way. You'd better shed those boots. They'll make an awful racket if we hit hard rock."

Again he felt like a small boy being told to do the most simple and obvious things. He shed the boots and was instantly aware of new difficulty. His feet were in ribbons from the terrible climb down and were chilblained by the shift in temperature as well. And now they had to contact sand which could have roasted eggs.

With the first steps he felt his feet beginning to blister and tears shot into his eyes from the pain. But Old Keno had also shed his boots and was striding easily forward, oblivious of this new agony. The old man, thought Moffat, would have walked through walls of fire with only an impatient backward glance to see if Moffat was coming.

"Are we close?" said Moffat at last and the words came out like rough pebbles, so achingly dry had his mouth become. Each gasp of air was like swallowing the plume on a blowtorch.

"No need to talk low," said Old Keno. "The wind's from them to us. They're camped by a running stream anyway and they can't hear above it. It'll be thirty degrees cooler where they are. This valley is like that. Hear it?"

Moffat couldn't but Old Keno was talking again, pointing to a tiny pinpoint, which was their fire, and the gleam, which was the spacecan, beside it.

"Cover all three from this side with your rifle. Don't shoot unless you have to. I'll circle and approach from the water side and challenge them. Don't plug me by mistake now!"

The disrespect in this made Constable Moffat wince. But he took station as requested. Lying across a frying hot rock with the night air broiling him, he laid the searing stock of the rifle against his cheek. He trained, as ordered, on the party about the fire.

He almost didn't care about what happened to himself anymore. He knew that the rock was burning him. He knew that the rifle barrel was raising a welt on his cheek. He felt some slight relief that his now-bleeding feet were off the ground. But he just didn't seem to care. There was the job to be done and that was all that mattered.

His body had been so beaten that his mind couldn't or wouldn't look at anything but the immediate present. All the concentration and will of his being was centered on this task. He would accomplish his purpose if it were the last purpose he would ever serve.

The three men in front of the fire were laughing, oblivious of any pursuit, certain in their security at least for the next few hours. Before dawn they would be out of the atmosphere and beyond reach. They had a big kettle in which they were boiling baybeef. From time to time one of them would pass another some particularly choice bit.

For an interminable while, it seemed to him (although in reality it was less than three minutes), Moffat waited. At length he heard Old Keno's voice.

"Keep yer hands clear, gents. I'm comin' in!" The three about the fire huddled, immobile as statues, clearly limned by the leaping flames. Thirty paces beyond them, into the circle of radiance, stepped Old Keno. His hands were swinging free, no weapon trained.

"I'll have to trouble you boys to come back and take your medicine," said Old Keno. "It ain't so much the diamonds, it's that guard. Human bein's come high up here."

"Frontier Police!" gasped the leader, starting to his feet. And then he realized what this meant—sure hanging!

"I wouldn't do anything foolish!" said Old Keno flatly.

The man wore a weapon, low and strapped down. "We're not bein' took. I reckon if you're a condemned enough fool to come after us all by yourself—"

The leader's hand, silhouetted in the firelight, flashed too fast to be followed.

There was a blend of roars, four shots! And then it was done.

Moffat had seen something he was never likely to forget. All three men had been on their feet. Old Keno's hands had been entirely free from his guns. The leader had drawn first and the other two had started to fire.

But Old Keno's left hand had stabbed across his body and his right had gone straight down and his three shots were like one blow. The leader's bullet went whining off on some lonesome errand amongst the rocks. Three men were dying there; three men had been shot before the leader had squeezed trigger.

And Constable Moffat's frozen, cut and blistered finger had tried to close to back up the play and Constable Moffat had not been able to fire! He stayed where he was, semi-paralyzed with the shock of what he had seen—three men shot in something like an eighth of a second.

The leader went down. Another man dropped into the fire. The third stood where he was, propped against a rock, eyes wide open and the firelight shining in them—stone dead.

Moffat looked at his hand. He had not even been able

to squeeze trigger. He, champion shot of the school, had not even been able to fire at his first live target when his companion was in danger!

On the verge of tears, Moffat came up from cover and walked toward the dying blaze. Old Keno was bending to retrieve their loot.

Moffat stepped into the ring of light. And then, of a sudden, a strange sensation came to him. It was like a yell inside his head. It was like an automatic switch being thrown. He knew he was in danger!

With the speed of a stabbed cat, young Moffat dropped to a knee, spinning on it toward the spacecan, drawing a rifle bead as he turned. He had not heard anything. But there stood a fat Asiatic in the passageway port, rifle leveled at Old Keno, about to shoot. He never got a chance.

Young Moffat fired from the hip and the bullet caught the fat one in the chest. His weapon exploded into the night. And then without looking at that target Moffat saw the second.

Under the shadow of the spacecan a man had come up, his arms full of firewood. This was falling now, halfway to the ground, and a gun was in his grip, aimed at Old Keno. The gun blazed. Moffat fired and the fifth man went down.

But he was not alone. Old Keno—the infallible, never-missing, always-beforehand Senior Constable of Ooglach—was flat on his face in the sand, motionless, victim of his own overconfidence.

Coming quickly to the spacecan port, young Moffat scanned the interior with his flash. There were five tumbled and evil-smelling bunks here. He glanced back to the fire, counting noses to make sure. Then he scouted wide, looking for strange tracks, and in a moment knew that they had the entire outfit. Not until then did he come back to Old Keno and there he knelt, turning the ancient patrolman over.

To see the wound and its extent it was necessary to remove Old Keno's shirt, for the bullet had apparently lightly creased his back.

It was cooler here by the side of the stream which, a few feet further, plumed two thousand feet into a chasm and which chilled the air in this cup. Young Moffat felt himself relaxing, beat up as he was. Old Keno missing such an obvious thing!

He had off the patched blue shirt and then rolled Keno to his face, fumbling for the wound. It was light; it was on the surface—

Suddenly Moffat stared. He came halfway to his feet and still stared. He took out his pocket flash and knelt eagerly beside the fallen man. His brows knit and then began to ease. Sudden laughter sprang from his lips, rose up the scale toward hysteria and turned aside into an honest bellow. What he had endured for this! *What* he had endured!

Young Constable Moffat sat down in the sand and held his sides. He laughed until his shoulders shook, until his breathing pounded, until his sides caved from labored wheezing. He laughed until the very sand around him danced. And then he looked—growing calmer and settling to a mere chuckle—back at the fallen man.

Moffat jumped up and went into the ship. Presently he

came back with a kit and began to patch. And in a very short while Old Keno was sitting groggily up, trying to piece together what had happened.

The young man watched him. Through Moffat's mind was flashing all he had gone through—the cold, the heat, the sharp rocks, the wreck. He thought of the fight when Old Keno had drawn and killed and he thought of the faculty Old Keno did not have. He had lasted and come out here.

"How much do you know of yourself?" said Moffat.

Old Keno stared in amazement and then, eyes shifting to the blue shirt and becoming conscious of his nakedness, slowly averted his gaze.

"Everything you know, I guess," he mumbled. "I didn't know it at first. I came up here for some reason I can't recall and the transport crashed near Meteorville. I thought I just had amnesia and I went to work in the bars as a guard.

"Then they made me marshal and finally the Frontier Patrol commissioned me a senior constable. Twenty years and I didn't know. Then I went down to Center City, where they built the big new prison. And they've got a gadget there to keep weapons from going in. I couldn't pass it. That's how I found out."

"Did anybody know?"

"I fell and when I came around I was okay. No, I don't think so. Why?"

"I think you were out longer than you thought," said Moffat. "By the way, did you ever read this sign on your back?"

"I tried with mirrors but I couldn't."

"Well, listen." Moffat studied it again before reading it aloud.

POLICE SPY
Pat. No. 4,625,726,867,094
THE BIG-AS-LIFE ROBOT CO.
"And twice as natural"

Motors: Carbon
Instruction: Police
Attachments: Infrared eyes
Chassis Type: R
"Our Robots Never Die"
Caution: DO NOT OIL!

Made in Detroit, Mich.
USA

There was silence for a moment. Old Keno looked scared and reached for his shirt. "You'll turn me in." He heaved a sigh. "I'm done."

Young Moffat grinned. "Nope. Because that isn't the only sign there. You were out a lot longer than you thought at Center City. They must have had time to send dispatches to the Frontier Patrol. Because there's another sign."

"Another?"

"Yep," said young Moffat with a jubilant upsurge. "It reads very short and very sweet."

To the recruit:

You'll only locate this if you can last, if you can't be fooled or if you're a better shot. Know then that you now send a dispatch to headquarters for your transfer and raise in rate. Well done, Senior Constable!

Thorpe
Commanding Section C

"I'm a trainer," said Old Keno.

"You showed up three," said Moffat. "Three that couldn't take it the hard way. And you almost killed me, Keno Martin. Froze me and broiled me and drained me of the last ounce. By golly, I never knew what I could stand until I came to Ooglach. And now . . . well, if they want to train a man the hard way it's all right with me."

"And I—" fumbled Old Keno.

"Martin, you're better than men in a lot of ways—heat, cold and energy. But of course your sixth sense doesn't exist. You'll have to watch for that. But you're still Senior Constable of Ooglach and I guess you'll last forever if you don't short-circuit from a slug.

"I replaced the fuse that bullet blew. You'd better keep some in your pockets. So they won't be retiring you, Keno, until you fall apart and according to your back, that won't be until forever arrives. Okay, Senior Constable?"

Old Keno became suddenly radiant. He looked at the boy before him and his smile grew proud. He put out his hand for a shake. "Okay, Senior Constable Moffat," he said.

They shook.

Battling Bolto

Battling Bolto

YOU hear some strange and amusing tales in the Intragalactic Survey, tales of the exiled and the damned. Men forgathered in some inhospitable system two jumps beyond forever from the nearest lighted window and far removed from the ordinary mediums of amusement, depend perforce upon themselves. There arises in every crew some champion teller of tales who, when company comes, is put forward by his fellows as a man of value and charm.

One would suppose such stories would be of high danger, sudden demise and new planets won, but this is never the case. The further the crew from its outflung base, the more intimately the yarns concern home.

Wandering around the stars, I have often been the target of "champion taletellers" and I wish that I had the memory to repeat one-hundredth of what we laughed and wept about at the Universe's end. Many of them, I suppose, in less glamorous and vigorous settings, told to men less abused by fates and the outer dark, would prove dull.

But whatever the setting, whatever the audience, I do not think any such charge could ever be leveled at Battling Bolto.

He was a huge ox of a man with a fitting sense of his own gullibility and weaknesses. He came from some system I will not name because he is badly wanted there—a common thing in the Survey, or how else would it ever recruit? He was fully seven feet tall and he had all the marks of one who had been raised on a gravity and a half. Earlier in the day, when our crews had boisterously met, he had amused us by manually hammering the dents from our hull, for he was a smith by trade and a smith he remained. His companions, when the fire was burning down, urged him on to tell his tale for us and after much bashful twisting and applications to the jug, the majority prevailed and he began to talk in a mellow roar which I am certain he believed to be quiet and fitting in this lonely, strange-starred night.

I wasn't cut out to be a rover (he began). It was a woman that did it. (He settled himself, took another drink and grinned into the fire.) I guess I never had much luck in keeping people from coming over me.

Down in Urgo Major, where I was born and raised, folks counted on me to become a pillar of the community and an example to the very young. And I would have if Aimee and the Professor had left my life alone.

Gentlemen, beware of professors. But they ain't a patch on women. I had a shop and I shoed a six-footed beast we had for a living and I mended people's pans and was all set to lead a comfortable and useful life when Aimee got to watching me in church. Pretty soon she was walking me home from church. And then she was expecting me to call Wednesday night. And the first thing I knew, I'd proposed to her. I can't rightly say just how it happened and for two or three weeks afterwards I kept wondering how it was I'd got engaged, and to this day I don't recall saying a word about it.

But we were posted up as likely bait for the parson and there I was. She'd come over me.

Wasn't any hurry about the marriage, but then I guess there isn't any hurry about anything down on our planet. Aimee was planning this and that and arranging the house Pop left me and everything seemed to be pretty smooth.

And then one day this spaceship landed.

Professor Crack McGowan he called himself. And the big banners he hung out said that he sold robots "for every purpose known to man." I figured this was going a little far. But I went down with the boys and we stood around and watched while he put on a show. It wasn't much. He had a robot that clanked around and gave a lecture and he had two men—humans—in the crew that shifted through the crowd handing out literature.

The robots was awful cheap but our planet is pretty poor and he didn't make many sales. And then I found my watch was gone.

Pop had give me that watch and I wasn't going to part with it amiable. I don't get mad very often but I got mad then. We'd been free of crime ever since the carnival came through and I figured it was the little goose-faced character that'd come through with the literature.

So I grabbed him, held him upside down in the air with one hand around his ankle and searched him.

I had just found my watch when I felt something hit me

that I figured must be part of the planet come loose. I got up and saw I was facing a man from some two-gravity world who had fists like elephants' feet and a face like a handsome ape. So we tangled.

Folks cheered around there and this Professor danced on the outskirts and the town cop held his peace. Chunks of turf as big as your head was flying like confetti and the display stand took on the happy appearance of a junkyard. We had a good time and then this character laid down and quit.

Well, an hour or so later when the doc had brought him around, Mike, our cop, agreed to let me go and I went back to the shop to wash off some blood and pieces of skin and hair. And here was this Professor waiting for me.

"I got a job for you," he says. "I'm partial to brawn and I got a good job. I am Professor Crack McGowan and I own a roaring good business that will let you see the Universe. Now how about it?"

Well, I explained I was happy and content but the more I explained, the higher his wages went and pretty soon I hear a cooing voice and there was Aimee. After that, all the dealing bypassed me cold and I found out a few days later, when we was sailing along at a couple light-years, that I'd been hired on as smith for six earth-years, a third of my pay going back to Aimee to compensate her for the wait. They'd come over me again.

But I didn't know anything yet. The bruiser I'd whipped and the little guy were gone and a couple humanoids helped in their place. I spent all my time back in the workshop turning out robot skins.

I never even had the run of the ship, which was a big one. She was called the *Opportunity,* which name, I might add, didn't include me. I knew she had some other workshops but they were always bolted down. She had a couple storerooms and they had things in them which looked like coffins and which I guessed must hold the robots he sold.

I made nothing but metal skins. The Professor would cart them off and that's all I knew about them. And this kept up for about two months of travel until I was sick of looking at my distorted reflection in curved plysteel, my face not being anything too wonderful to begin with.

And then this Professor comes back and he tells me to start on a new, big skin of a certain design and size of a new metal. I didn't ask any questions. He was sort of a hard man to talk to—little and scrawny and always in a hurry and a lot more glib than I care to meet in my fellow travelers. So I made the skin. Had a little trouble with materials. Kind of faceplate he wanted wasn't aboard so I tore up the only spacesuit.

"Now," he says when I'm done with it, "put it on."

"Put it on?" I said. "Why?"

So I put it on. He'd come over me again. I sure felt silly. It had joints for all my joints and a visor in the "face" that you could look out of but not into and a goofy helmet on it, and when I saw myself in the glass I almost got scared. Gruesome.

"Now," he says, "that's fine. We land in about three hours so you might as well stay dressed."

"Why dressed?" I said.

So I stayed dressed and we landed.

It was a pretty planet, mostly blue grass and orange trees and a sprinkling of humans in the crowd.

Before he opened the port, the Professor said, "Now I want you to go out there and move around and demonstrate things. It's just a joke and we'll take off your helmet at the end of the performance and they'll all laugh. So go outside."

Well, I went outside in this tin suit, feeling like seven kinds of idiot, and clanked around. And the people all looked interested and polite because it was a religious holiday and they didn't have anything else to do anyway and spaceships from strange places were unusual in these parts. Then the Professor puts up a stand and his two humanoids begin to spread this banner. It read:

BATTLING BOLTO

The Robot Boxing Champion
of the Universe and Sub-dimensions

$10,000 PRIZE TO ANYONE STAYING
WITH HIM TWO ROUNDS!

Well, robots were common enough, even if they were expensive as the dickens, and a boxing robot wasn't too much for me to wonder about, and so I stood and stared at the space lock waiting for this wonder to appear. And then I felt the Professor's hand on my arm and, by golly, I was Battling Bolto! He'd come over me again.

The hicks stood around and the crowd got bigger, and the Professor put on a spiel about his special farm robots and people were real interested.

"Now, gentlemen," said the Professor in a braying voice, "I have planned a little exhibition just to show you how magnificent our product really is. You all know that most robots are delicate, that they have a poor sense of direction, timing and balance, but, gentlemen, this is not true of our product! Battling Bolto will prove to you how superior our products really are."

The humanoids were lining up coffinlike boxes and taking the lids off and a whole line of inert robots were displayed beside the ship.

"Our robots sell for one thousand dollars. One thousand paltry dollars, full price. Ten measly little hundred-dollar bills! You can't lose. Our nearest competitor sells this same type robot, of infinitely inferior skill, for twenty-one thousand dollars. Save that middleman profit. Save the manufacturer's squeeze. Save the freight! Buy one of my fine, class A robots, guaranteed forever. . . . Step right up here, young man. What's your name?"

A great big hulk of a kid had been hustled out from town and several of the leading citizens were pushing him ahead.

"Jasper Wilkins," he says.

"Jasper Wilkins!" says the Professor, as though that was the finest name he'd ever heard. "Now, Jasper, are you sure you want to go two rounds with Battling Bolto?"

"He's the country champion!" yelled his backers.

"Yep. Guess I do," said Jasper. And they began to make a ring for us.

Well, I was just coming to life. All of a sudden I was suspicious that the Professor wasn't going to tell anybody about my not being a robot. And I figured that going up against this Jasper Wilkins was pretty unfair. He was bigger'n me but I was wearing plysteel, thirty proof, and I had on gloves that would have gone through a hull. And I was trying to figure out what would happen if I called the Professor down when I felt somebody putting a great big pair of boxing gloves on me. And somebody else was shoving me from behind. And the Professor says sternly, in a monotonous voice, "Bolto, go in and fight, young man. *Ugh.*"

Right about then I started to say my piece, but this young Jasper Wilkins was eager. He let me have one that almost broke my neck and after that things got blurred.

The crowd kept screaming and the face of young Wilkins kept getting in the way of my punches and the ground shook and then there he was, down for the count before the first round was done.

His friends picked him up and the Professor started his talk. I was to hear that talk pretty often.

"Here's five hundred dollars for the young man because of his pluck. Nobody can beat Battling Bolto. But Battling Bolto is only an oversize example of our wares. They are all reliable. They are all deadly. They do your work and fight your battles and slave for you twenty-four hours a day. Unless you have their code, they will not work for you nor move. Now step right up. . . ."

Well, he sold thirty robots. "There's the directions. Take them into a field and practice pitching your voice and finally you will have them all at your command. First, set their receivers to respond and then master their actions. Don't experiment near a crowd because they may go berserk until you know their management. There you are, sir. Cart away the box."

The humanoids nailed on the lids and handed them out and then we were in the air again.

I waited in the passage behind the control room until the Professor came out.

"I quit," I said. "Take me back where I came from or I'll beat in your skull. I don't play that way and I won't ever again. Now do we understand each other or shall I argue it out in my own way?"

It would have been pretty simple to drive him through the floor with one blow on the top of his head. I wish I had.

"My valiant friend," he said, "look before you leap—or I should say, beware of whom you seek to destroy. I am very much afraid that you were slow in understanding my explanations of your job. I told you all about it and it's in your contract plain as day."

"Just so, put me down where I can get passage home," I said. "You've got plenty of robots. Fix one of them so it can box."

"Alas," said the Professor, "robots are not sufficiently well balanced to follow that manly art."

"But you told those people back there— The robots you sold them are supposed—"

"Alas again, my handy smith, not only do those robots know nothing of boxing, they are woefully ignorant of other things as well."

"But you said—"

"Friend, what I say does not alter the fact that we have just sold thirty empty shells. They do not work, neither do they spin. You made all there is to them. You should know."

"Hey! The Galactic Police will hear of that!"

"In the years to come. But space is wide, smith, space is wide."

A horrible thought hit me. "Those robots you sold on my own planet . . . were they . . ."

"Alas, 'tis true. They were but empty shells. And I fear, smith, that you delivered several yourself just before we left. So I shouldn't think about going home just now."

I was getting hotter than the tin suit made me. "How many did you sell back there?"

"Eighteen, my friend."

"Give me the eighteen thousand and set me down so that I can go home and repay my friends!"

He thought about this for a while and then his face got bright. "Tell you what, smith. If you'll just fight eighteen fights for me, I'll pay you a bonus of a thousand dollars for every fight. Then you can have your wages and go. No one will have seen you. Only your home planet will suspect you and with their money refunded they will think you are at least a hero who has saved the day. That will give you ten thousand in wages, eighteen thousand in—"

"It would take me two years to earn that much in wages," I said. "I won't stay."

"Ah, no. Your wages have just been raised. Now will you go back to your shop and let me to my own work?"

He left me. After a while I went back, took off the robot suit and picked up my hammer. He'd come over me again.

Well, I hate to tell of the next few months. We were in a close pack of stars and we could make a lot of stops and I sweated in the shop to keep up with the demand. I was ashamed of myself every blow I struck with my hammer, but what else could I do? I wasn't going to be an exile forever and a smith that could make eighteen thousand on our planet in half a lifetime hasn't been born, what with the galactic taxes and the tithe to the lord that owns the atomic launching site there. So I squirmed but I worked. And I cussed myself but I fought.

I could weep when I think of the poor country lads I messed up in the next few months. Having metal doesn't completely protect you. You rattle around in it. And it's sometimes so golblamed hot you could cry. So now and then I'd get jolted so hard I'd get mad and then they'd be a week bringing some kid around.

But I stuck it. I had myself kidded then that I desperately adored this Aimee and I was homesick for my own forge. And I battered away at the fake robots. And the Professor ballyhooed away at the hicks. And I pummeled all comers. And then we hit Mondyke.

Maybe you've heard of Mondyke. It's a big planet, covered with grassland and lakes and no seas, and the corn grows about ninety feet high, more or less, and they've got a monopoly on yeastfood stocks over about five systems. They don't grow any place but Mondyke and they swell up to a ton of food from a two-pound chunk, given water. Well, anyway, that's what they told me.

So we landed there because the Professor figured this was

a big haul. It was my seventeenth trip but he said that if we sold a hundred robots he'd call it square and I could drop off at the next stop beyond. Well, this suited me fine. I was all set to get back to Aimee and my forge and sextet horseshoes and I was really glad to land and see the initial spiel come off.

The Professor, he really laid the thing on. He let 'em have both barrels. He showed them a lot of electronic tricks and "robot parts" and then he come down to me, Battling Bolto.

Well, I'd never seen him come on it so heavy before. He let loose on the big mob that came out from the town like he was running for galactic tax collector. He promised them everything except heaven. And then he wound it up grand.

It was a beautiful day, the grass all green and a lot of fleecy clouds up above just like our planet, and women with picnic baskets and kids running around raising the dickens and men looking wise and explaining electronics to each other in terms that would sure surprise an engineer, and the Professor coming down hard about me. I can see it all like it was yesterday.

He had the humanoids in robot skins now and they were passing out literature.

"And Battling Bolto, ladies and gentlemen, is the supreme combat champion in all forms of warfare over anything which may be met in the *entire* universe!" He was safe there. The biggest animal they had on Mondyke was a stork. "And as a gratis demonstration of his skill, ladies and gentlemen, Battling Bolto will guarantee to go two rounds with anything you can bring before him. Anything, ladies and gentlemen. Now, if there is some young man in the crowd who believes himself a master of robots and a terror to mere machines, let him step fearlessly forward now and challenge the title holder of the Universe in all forms of physical combat!"

A couple young bucks began to edge up, husky kids, one of them bigger than me, plenty strong from throwing tractors around. I figured it was going to be an easy fight. And then an old geezer in a straw hat comes up and holds a consultation with the Professor.

"I can't wait long!" said the Professor in a loud voice.

"It won't be long!" said the old geezer. And he goes back to his friends and they roar off in a truck. The Professor had no more'n started to fill in the breach when back they come.

The truck springs give a little and the next thing I knew comes a robot, walking heavy. He was about my height, but he had a lot more beam and head. He was a farm robot and as tough as space beef.

I started to protest but I caught the Professor's eye. This was my chance. And around comes this here robot, walking slow. He give me the creeps and I all of a sudden saw how a lot of other guys had felt.

"This here," said the old geezer for the crowd, "is a thirty-five-thousand-dollar utility Workster. He can wrastle horses if any durn fool'd let him. And I got me ten thousand dollars on the side that he can lick your chunk of scrap metal hands down in two rounds."

"He has the offered prize," said the Professor, sizing up this Workster. It was a new model, a kind that hadn't been in circulation before. And it sure looked like it had good balance.

"Sir," said the Professor, "the side bet is made. Now, ladies and gentlemen, the terror of the Universe, Battling Bolto, will meet his opponent fair and square and no holds barred. And we take no responsibility for damage to anything. So stand clear and make a ring and let the CHAMPEEEEEEN OF THE UNIVERSE *swing*!"

I sure didn't like the looks of this but I stepped in anyway. What else could I do? This was going to be my last fight.

The Workster's eyes kept flashing up and glowing and he creaked and clanked as he got his hinges automatically oiled. He looked pretty awesome, standing there, no soft spot anywhere to be seen. And then the Professor came down with the gloves.

"No you don't," said the old geezer. "This is a barehanded scrap and my robot needs everything he can get. Let's go!"

The crowd backed him and the Professor gave me my phony command and I stepped up, looking cagey, trying to figure out how this here robot would go to it. And then, WHAM! I sailed backwards about twenty feet and hit hard enough to knock my teeth loose.

I got up groggy, listening to the crowd jeer. And this confounded robot was right on top of me, kicking!

I got up and I went down. I got up again, took a couple hard ones that dented my chest and stayed up. I spit out some blood and began to use footwork. And in about two minutes I found that this robot could do everything but dance. He couldn't do that. And it cost him the fight. I could get back of him quicker than he could turn and I hit him until my arms were numb to my neck. And then his head came off.

I hit him until my arms were numb to my neck.
And then his head came off.

It made a tinkly sound. Springs whirred out straight. Tubes popped as they blew. And there was an arc and a spiral of blue smoke out of his joints. He stood there, teetering. And then he went down like a pile of scrap metal falling from fifty feet.

"My robot!" wailed the old geezer. "It'll cost ten thousand to put him together."

If he ever finds the parts, I growled, mad.

"Now that this little exhibition has established the superiority of my robots—" began the Professor.

"Wait, wait!" said somebody on the edge of the crowd. And a big truck went off in a tear while a young guy came up and argued with the old geezer. Finally the old guy seemed to agree and they approached the Professor.

"We want another fight," said the old geezer, "and Barney here has got another robot. If you'd care to make the wager . . ."

Professor McGowan did. The truck came back and I looked up from where I had been sitting, trying to look like a robot and still catch my breath, to see the most confoundedly big piece of metal I'd seen this side of a war tank.

This robot was not just big. He was a walking horror. He had spikes all over him.

"What is this?" cried the Professor angrily.

"This is an INDESTRUCTO dam builder," said the old geezer jumping about. "It works underwater against currents and it drives piles with its fists." He was capering about waving his hat. "You said *anything*. And we forgot all about our engineer corps machines. You'll have to fight it. You said you would."

Well, I felt pretty gray. This thing was really a robot. It was a pile-driving tank which put logs in place with one hand and drove them in with the other. But it had eyes and was self-animated and had treads. So there we were.

I was about to pull a blown-out-fuse trick when I caught a glare from the Professor.

The young guy—and I saw now that he had an engineer uniform on—was pointing me out carefully to INDESTRUCTO.

"Log. You drive. Log. You drive," he was saying.

"Robot, you fight," the Professor said to me.

They made the ring again. The thing's treads sank in the soft grass and he churned at me. He was used to battle currents. Nothing could knock him off his feet. I was already numb from the first fight. But I started in there anyway. What could I do?

Well, I took a swipe at him from the side and he wheeled. I went around and took another swipe and he wheeled again. One hand was pawing out with yard-long fingers, ready to wrap around my body, and the other was a natural fist, weighing a couple hundred pounds, ready to come down on me when the fingers connected.

I kept going around back and hitting. It was like trying to knock an anvil in half.

It was such a pleasant day. And the crowd was so pleased. And the hand kept reaching for me and the fist stayed poised.

I wondered how proof I'd made my own headpiece. I began to question my own forge work. And I kept circling, kept hitting futile blows. And the time for the two rounds sped along.

Finally I figured I had my chance. I saw where the skull turret joined the body and I saw that it had some folds of metal to let it go up and down. If I dared get in and up that close I might possibly make one hard blow count. It would be like putting my fist through a half-inch of steel, but my fist was steel shod too.

So I dived.

So it caught me.

So the fist came down!

The only thing which kept me alive was busting three of its fingers off. But the hammer hit me a glance on the chest and then I knew no more.

I must have been flung a long way. Something like a billiard ball. And I must have hit the hull of the ship because there was a dent in it. But where I was it was cool and pleasant, out of the sun, and there I was content to stay.

Nobody had come near me, and the crowd was wild. I thought they were silly cheering a robot until I got to my elbows and looked between some legs. And there I beheld the strangest sight I ever hope to see.

A ten-foot robot was dancing around INDESTRUCTO like a foosha native around a missionary. My brains were beginning to straighten out a bit now. I had been partly conscious, enough so to hear the clanging steps of something coming out of the ship above me.

Somebody was leaping around watching and holding a sheaf of bills which looked like a bet big enough to buy a star. The Professor was bellowing commands into a funny box and the battle royal was raging.

INDESTRUCTO kept wheeling but the ten-foot giant kept dancing. And every now and then the Professor's robot would dive in and twist another piece of metal out of the engineer machine. INDESTRUCTO began to look like he'd been machine-gunned.

Pieces of turf were flying through the air. The place was torn up like it had been plowed. And the whir of those machines was so quiet under the scream of the crowd that it gave me the creeps.

And then the engineer pile driver, the late, lamented INDESTRUCTO, the victor over BATTLING BOLTO, tilted over and went down. One tread spun for a moment and then the ten-foot giant tore it off and threw it away.

The Professor barked new commands. The robot turned and clanged up the ladder and into the ship. The humanoids in their suits began to pass out the boxes. The old geezer sat down and began to mourn about how he'd mortgaged the farm, and I lay there and blinked.

After a while I got up and went into the ship. I walked stiff and it wasn't an act.

The last of the boxes were sold. And the Professor was giving his final caution about training the robots in an open field first and some of the purchasers were trying to pry off the lids they'd just seen nailed on, and all in all, brothers, it was time to go.

"Sorry I lost," I said to the Professor.

"Why, as for that," that gentleman said, "I expected you

would sooner or later. But you gave me a wonderful scheme and I had to have time to build some real robot fighters that I wouldn't be in any risk about. So, my valiant smith, we part."

"Wait a minute," I yelled. "You can't gyp me!"

"Can't I?" he said.

"Those people out there would kill me if they knew. Look here, 'Professor' McGowan, I know what you look like and the Galactic Police will be pretty interested in an accurate description of you and your ways. You can't get away with this. I'll make you known to every planet in the whole Universe. I'll see that you're hunted down. I'll—"

"Oh, will you?" he said. And he reached up to his face and he throws a spring catch and there I am, staring into a set of wheels and tubes behind the lowered plate. It gave me a terrible turn.

And a voice from one of the staterooms I'd never seen open barked, "Outside with them both!"

I heard a whir and then a clang and I looked up to see ten feet of giant robot getting set to knock me fifty miles. I back-flipped out through the port and hit in the turf and the McGowan robot hit beside me with a clang.

The ship's lock closed and I grabbed at its tail. I'd been come over again. It was gone.

The man paused and took a sorrowful drink. And then, on urging, finally resumed his tale.

"What did they do? Heck, what else could they do? There I was, a man posing as a robot with a robot posing as a man. What did they do with me? They sent me into the galactic prison, of course, and I worked for a long, long time on those mines.

"What happened to whoever it was that was really in charge? Well, I don't know, to tell the truth. But I have my opinions."

From his jacket he pulled something he must have used as a weapon. "I saved a piece of it and made it up pretty-like while I worked in the mines. He'd come over me so many times, it was only fair to come over *him* just once. What is it? Why, it's his right steering tube, of course.

"And I drove my fist through the pressure hull for good measure. Came off awful easy. Often wondered where he crashed. Repaired it? How could he? The only spacesuit aboard the *Opportunity* I used to make Battling Bolto's faceplate from, it being the only stuff anywhere in stock. Besides, all the air was out of the ship. You ever seen him in orbit anyplace, you fellows?"

I told him no because you don't find a ship once it is lost in space. And I asked him was this the reason he was in the Survey now.

"Why, no," he said. "Truth to tell, they let me keep my McGowan robot, so I had a 'manager.' We were on circuit for years after that as Battling Bolto. Selling empty tin skins, of course."

Story Preview

NOW that you've just ventured through some of the captivating tales in the Stories from the Golden Age collection by L. Ron Hubbard, turn the page and enjoy a preview of *One Was Stubborn*. Old Shellback's the most stubborn man in the universe: he's simply unwilling to watch the universe crumble and vanish, the product of an alleged agreement among the living to think it away. When Shellback won't budge, he throws a wrench into the works.

One Was Stubborn

I was so groggy when I stepped off the conveyer belt and grabbed the scoop which lifted up to the medical department level that I didn't even see a crazy college student swing off Level 20 in his antique Airable Swishabout—one of those things with signs over the dents saying, "Eve, Here's Your Atom," and "Ten Tubes All Disintegrating," and "Hey, Babe, didn't we meet on Mars?" You know the menace. Well, one of those blasted straight at me and I didn't even have time to duck—and I probably couldn't have anyway, thanks to my rheumatism.

And if I had been startled before, I was prostrate now. That Swishabout rattled to the right and left and above and below and was gone. I'd passed all the way through it!

I was almost scared to let go of the bucket and step out on the Eye Level for fear the invisible walk was not only invisible but also not there!

Somehow I hauled myself up to the sorting psycher while the beam calculators sized me up and then, when the flasher had blinked "Dr. Flerry" as its decision for me, I managed to sink down on the sofa which whisked me into his office.

The nurse smiled pleasantly and said, "Nervous disability is quite easy to correct and Dr. Flerry is expert. Please be calm."

"I haven't got any nervous disability," I said. "I came up here to get tested for some glasses."

She looked at one of those confounded charts that the sorting psycher forwards ahead of the patient, and when I saw her finger come down to "Stubborn" I knew she'd nod. She did. A thoroughly unmanageable young woman.

"You haven't been brought to an eye doctor," she said. "Dr. Flerry treats nervous disability only, as you must know."

"I came for an eye test," I said, "and I'm going to get an eye test. I don't give a flimdoodle what that blathery card says; it's *eyes.* Do you think a machine knows more about me than I do?"

"Sometimes a machine does. Now please don't get upset."

"I'm not upset. I guess I know when I need glasses and when I don't need glasses. And if I want to be tested for glasses, I pretty well guess I'll be tested for glasses!"

"You," she said, "are obviously a stubborn sort of fellow."

"I guess," I said, "that I am the most stubborn fellow in this city if not in this whole country."

"Don't tell me," she said.

Well, I don't know why, but I felt a little better after that. And shortly, Dr. Flerry buzzered me into his inner office. He was one of these disgusting young fellows who think they know so much about the human body that they themselves can't be human.

"Now be calm," he said, "and tell me just what the trouble is." He seemed to be in a sort of ecstatic state and he didn't seem to take me seriously enough.

"I won't be calm," I said, "and I don't have to tell you what the trouble is. You've got a psycher chart there that will tell you all about me even down to my last wart."

"Yes," he said, "you do have a wart. I shall have Dr. Dremster remove it before you go."

"You won't touch any wart of mine," I said. "I came in here to get a pair of glasses, and by the Eternal, I'll get them if I have to sit here all night."

I guess I had him there, for he sat and stared at me for some little time before he replied.

Finally he said, "Now just what is making you nervous?"

"I am *not* nervous!" I shouted. "I want glasses!"

"Ah," he said. And then he sat back and pushed his head against a pad so the mechanical chair arm would put a lighted cigarette in his mouth. "My dear fellow, tell me just why you need a pair of glasses."

"Because I need them, that's why!"

"Reading glasses?"

"Reading glasses!" I said. "I never read any of the bilge the papers are ordered to publish."

"Then you watch the televisor quite a bit?"

"I wouldn't turn one of those things on for a million dollars. What do you ever hear but advertising and smoky bands, and what do you see but girls with legs? Bah!" I guess I was telling him now.

"Ah," he said and thumped back with an elbow so that his chair's arm would pour him a glass of water. "But you don't need glasses to talk to people."

"I never talk to people. I never talk to anybody except my

wife and I don't talk to her and she doesn't listen to me any more than I listen to her. She never says three words a week to me anyway." Which is the way things should be, of course.

"What, may I ask, is your business?"

"You've got a nerve to ask, but for your information I haven't got any business. I retired off my farm about four years ago and I haven't spent a happy hour since."

"Ah," he said.

"Don't sit there saying 'Ah' like an idiot," I said. "Get busy and fit me with a pair of glasses."

"You haven't said why you needed them. You can have them of course, but to give them to you I'll have to know just what sort of glasses you mean. What convinced you that you should have them?"

I could see that I had scared Dr. Flerry into being polite to me, so I told him that I had seen a pair of legs without a torso and had first missed and then seen one of the Medical Center domes and how that crazy college student had run right through me.

Well, if Dr. Flerry hadn't stopped laughing when he did I guess we would have mixed it up right then.

"What's so funny?" I demanded.

"Why, my dear fellow," said Dr. Flerry, "you don't need any glasses. If you ever paid any attention to the newspapers or the televisors or talked to anyone, you'd understand what is happening."

"And what," said I, "is happening?"

GLOSSARY

STORIES FROM THE GOLDEN AGE *reflect the words and expressions used in the 1930s and 1940s, adding unique flavor and authenticity to the tales. While a character's speech may often reflect regional origins, it also can convey attitudes common in the day. So that readers can better grasp such cultural and historical terms, uncommon words or expressions of the era, the following glossary has been provided.*

---

alpha: first in order of brightness.

ballyhoo: to attract the attention of customers by raising a clamor. The ballyhoo is a sophisticated "commercial," usually illustrated with quick appearances by the performers given to draw a crowd to see a show.

bead, drawing a rifle: variation of "to draw a bead on"; taking aim at. This term alludes to the *bead,* a small metal knob on a firearm used as a front sight.

bilge: worthless talk; nonsense.

blathery: unsubstantial; rotten; trashy.

braying: uttering loudly and harshly.

bucks: men, especially strong or spirited young men.

chilblain: inflammation, followed by itchy irritation on hands, feet or ears that have been exposed to moist cold.

coming over or **come over:** deceiving or taking advantage of someone.

complection: complexion; general appearance or nature.

constable: a law enforcement officer.

crookt: crooked; bent.

ergs: units of energy.

Eternal, by the: used to express surprise or emphasis; *the Eternal* refers to God.

flimdoodle, don't give a: variation of "don't give a hoot"; to not care about something at all.

flimflam: to trick, deceive, swindle or cheat.

gibbous: of the moon, between the half-moon and the full moon.

G-men: government men; agents of the Federal Bureau of Investigation.

golblamed: goddamned; used as an expression of anger, disgust, etc.

hicks: people regarded as gullible or unsophisticated.

horizon blue and gold: a uniform; a field uniform the color of horizon blue, a variable color averaging a light greenish blue to blue, with gold buttons.

hummocks: ridges or hills of ice in an ice field.

ill-starred: doomed to end in failure or disaster.

import: 1. consequence or importance; matter. 2. meaning; implication.

limned: outlined in clear detail; delineated.

mackinaw: a thick heavy woolen cloth, usually with a plaid design.

mean: inferior in grade or quality.

patch on, isn't a: to not be as good as someone or something else.

physiognomy: the features of somebody's face, especially when they are used as indicators of that person's character or temperament.

plugged: (of a coin) with the center removed and replaced with a worthless metal.

proof: 1. tested or proved strength, as of armor. 2. capable of resisting harm, injury or damage.

quarters, at: at a proper or assigned station or place, as for officers and crew on a warship.

Scheherazade: the female narrator of *The Arabian Nights,* who during one thousand and one adventurous nights saved her life by entertaining her husband, the king, with stories.

shod: covered for protection, strength or ornament.

subscriptions: funds raised through sums of money pledged.

tramp: a freight vessel that does not run regularly between fixed ports, but takes a cargo wherever shippers desire.

L. Ron Hubbard in the Golden Age of Pulp Fiction

In writing an adventure story
a writer has to know that he is adventuring
for a lot of people who cannot.
The writer has to take them here and there
about the globe and show them
excitement and love and realism.
As long as that writer is living the part of an
adventurer when he is hammering
the keys, he is succeeding with his story.

Adventuring is a state of mind.
If you adventure through life, you have a
good chance to be a success on paper.

Adventure doesn't mean globe-trotting,
exactly, and it doesn't mean great deeds.
Adventuring is like art.
You have to live it to make it real.

—L. Ron Hubbard

L. Ron Hubbard and American Pulp Fiction

BORN March 13, 1911, L. Ron Hubbard lived a life at least as expansive as the stories with which he enthralled a hundred million readers through a fifty-year career.

Originally hailing from Tilden, Nebraska, he spent his formative years in a classically rugged Montana, replete with the cowpunchers, lawmen and desperadoes who would later people his Wild West adventures. And lest anyone imagine those adventures were drawn from vicarious experience, he was not only breaking broncs at a tender age, he was also among the few whites ever admitted into Blackfoot society as a bona fide blood brother. While if only to round out an otherwise rough and tumble youth, his mother was that rarity of her time—a thoroughly educated woman—who introduced her son to the classics of Occidental literature even before his seventh birthday.

But as any dedicated L. Ron Hubbard reader will attest, his world extended far beyond Montana. In point of fact, and as the son of a United States naval officer, by the age of eighteen he had traveled over a quarter of a million miles. Included therein were three Pacific crossings to a then still mysterious Asia, where he ran with the likes of Her British Majesty's agent-in-place

L. Ron Hubbard, left, at Congressional Airport, Washington, DC, 1931, with members of George Washington University flying club.

for North China, and the last in the line of Royal Magicians from the court of Kublai Khan. For the record, L. Ron Hubbard was also among the first Westerners to gain admittance to forbidden Tibetan monasteries below Manchuria, and his photographs of China's Great Wall long graced American geography texts.

Upon his return to the United States and a hasty completion of his interrupted high school education, the young Ron Hubbard entered George Washington University. There, as fans of his aerial adventures may have heard, he earned his wings as a pioneering barnstormer at the dawn of American aviation. He also earned a place in free-flight record books for the longest sustained flight above Chicago. Moreover, as a roving reporter for *Sportsman Pilot* (featuring his first professionally penned articles), he further helped inspire a generation of pilots who would take America to world airpower.

Immediately beyond his sophomore year, Ron embarked on the first of his famed ethnological expeditions, initially to then untrammeled Caribbean shores (descriptions of which would later fill a whole series of West Indies mystery-thrillers). That the Puerto Rican interior would also figure into the future of Ron Hubbard stories was likewise no accident. For in addition to cultural studies of the island, a 1932–33

LRH expedition is rightly remembered as conducting the first complete mineralogical survey of a Puerto Rico under United States jurisdiction.

There was many another adventure along this vein: As a lifetime member of the famed Explorers Club, L. Ron Hubbard charted North Pacific waters with the first shipboard radio direction finder, and so pioneered a long-range navigation system universally employed until the late twentieth century. While not to put too fine an edge on it, he also held a rare Master Mariner's license to pilot any vessel, of any tonnage in any ocean.

Capt. L. Ron Hubbard in Ketchikan, Alaska, 1940, on his Alaskan Radio Experimental Expedition, the first of three voyages conducted under the Explorers Club flag.

Yet lest we stray too far afield, there is an LRH note at this juncture in his saga, and it reads in part:

"I started out writing for the pulps, writing the best I knew, writing for every mag on the stands, slanting as well as I could."

To which one might add: His earliest submissions date from the summer of 1934, and included tales drawn from true-to-life Asian adventures, with characters roughly modeled on British/American intelligence operatives he had known in Shanghai. His early Westerns were similarly peppered with details drawn from personal experience. Although therein lay a first hard lesson from the often cruel world of the pulps. His first Westerns were soundly rejected as lacking the authenticity of a Max Brand yarn (a particularly frustrating comment given L. Ron Hubbard's Westerns came straight from his Montana homeland, while Max Brand was a mediocre New York poet named Frederick Schiller Faust, who turned out implausible six-shooter tales from the terrace of an Italian villa).

Nevertheless, and needless to say, L. Ron Hubbard persevered and soon earned a reputation as among the most publishable names in pulp fiction, with a ninety percent placement rate of first-draft manuscripts. He was also among the most prolific, averaging between seventy and a hundred thousand words a month. Hence the rumors that L. Ron Hubbard had redesigned a typewriter for faster keyboard action and pounded out manuscripts on a continuous roll of butcher paper to save the precious seconds it took to insert a single sheet of paper into manual typewriters of the day.

That all L. Ron Hubbard stories did not run beneath said byline is yet another aspect of pulp fiction lore. That is, as publishers periodically rejected manuscripts from top-drawer authors if only to avoid paying top dollar, L. Ron Hubbard and company just as frequently replied with submissions under various pseudonyms. In Ron's case, the

A Man of Many Names

Between 1934 and 1950, L. Ron Hubbard authored more than fifteen million words of fiction in more than two hundred classic publications. To supply his fans and editors with stories across an array of genres and pulp titles, he adopted fifteen pseudonyms in addition to his already renowned L. Ron Hubbard byline.

Winchester Remington Colt
Lt. Jonathan Daly
Capt. Charles Gordon
Capt. L. Ron Hubbard
Bernard Hubbel
Michael Keith
Rene Lafayette
Legionnaire 148
Legionnaire 14830
Ken Martin
Scott Morgan
Lt. Scott Morgan
Kurt von Rachen
Barry Randolph
Capt. Humbert Reynolds

list included: Rene Lafayette, Captain Charles Gordon, Lt. Scott Morgan and the notorious Kurt von Rachen—supposedly on the lam for a murder rap, while hammering out two-fisted prose in Argentina. The point: While L. Ron Hubbard as Ken Martin spun stories of Southeast Asian intrigue, LRH as Barry Randolph authored tales of romance on the Western range—which, stretching between a dozen genres is how he came to stand among the two hundred elite authors providing close to a million tales through the glory days of American Pulp Fiction.

L. Ron Hubbard, circa 1930, at the outset of a literary career that would finally span half a century.

In evidence of exactly that, by 1936 L. Ron Hubbard was literally leading pulp fiction's elite as president of New York's American Fiction Guild. Members included a veritable pulp hall of fame: Lester "Doc Savage" Dent, Walter "The Shadow" Gibson, and the legendary Dashiell Hammett—to cite but a few.

Also in evidence of just where L. Ron Hubbard stood within his first two years on the American pulp circuit: By the spring of 1937, he was ensconced in Hollywood, adopting a Caribbean thriller for Columbia Pictures, remembered today as *The Secret of Treasure Island.* Comprising fifteen thirty-minute episodes, the L. Ron Hubbard screenplay led to the most profitable matinée serial in Hollywood history. In accord with Hollywood culture, he was thereafter continually called upon

The 1937 Secret of Treasure Island, *a fifteen-episode serial adapted for the screen by L. Ron Hubbard from his novel,* Murder at Pirate Castle.

to rewrite/doctor scripts—most famously for long-time friend and fellow adventurer Clark Gable.

In the interim—and herein lies another distinctive chapter of the L. Ron Hubbard story—he continually worked to open Pulp Kingdom gates to up-and-coming authors. Or, for that matter, anyone who wished to write. It was a fairly unconventional stance, as markets were already thin and competition razor sharp. But the fact remains, it was an L. Ron Hubbard hallmark that he vehemently lobbied on behalf of young authors—regularly supplying instructional articles to trade journals, guest-lecturing to short story classes at George Washington University and Harvard, and even founding his own creative writing competition. It was established in 1940, dubbed the Golden Pen, and guaranteed winners both New York representation and publication in *Argosy.*

But it was John W. Campbell Jr.'s *Astounding Science Fiction* that finally proved the most memorable LRH vehicle. While every fan of L. Ron Hubbard's galactic epics undoubtedly knows the story, it nonetheless bears repeating: By late 1938, the pulp publishing magnate of Street & Smith was determined to revamp *Astounding Science Fiction* for broader readership. In particular, senior editorial director F. Orlin Tremaine called for stories with a stronger *human element.* When acting editor John W. Campbell balked, preferring his spaceship-driven tales, Tremaine enlisted Hubbard. Hubbard, in turn, replied with the genre's first truly *character-driven* works, wherein heroes are pitted not against bug-eyed monsters but the mystery and majesty of deep space itself—and thus was launched the Golden Age of Science Fiction.

The names alone are enough to quicken the pulse of any science fiction aficionado, including LRH friend and protégé, Robert Heinlein, Isaac Asimov, A. E. van Vogt and Ray Bradbury. Moreover, when coupled with LRH stories of fantasy, we further come to what's rightly been described as the foundation of every modern tale of horror: L. Ron Hubbard's immortal *Fear.* It was rightly proclaimed by Stephen King as one of the very few works to genuinely warrant that overworked term "classic"—as in: *"This is a classic tale of creeping, surreal menace and horror. . . . This is one of the really, really good ones."*

L. Ron Hubbard, 1948, among fellow science fiction luminaries at the World Science Fiction Convention in Toronto.

To accommodate the greater body of L. Ron Hubbard fantasies, Street & Smith inaugurated *Unknown*—a classic pulp if there ever was one, and wherein readers were soon thrilling to the likes of *Typewriter in the Sky* and *Slaves of Sleep* of which Frederik Pohl would declare: *"There are bits and pieces from Ron's work that became part of the language in ways that very few other writers managed."*

And, indeed, at J. W. Campbell Jr.'s insistence, Ron was regularly drawing on themes from the Arabian Nights and so introducing readers to a world of genies, jinn, Aladdin and Sinbad—all of which, of course, continue to float through cultural mythology to this day.

At least as influential in terms of post-apocalypse stories was L. Ron Hubbard's 1940 *Final Blackout*. Generally acclaimed as the finest anti-war novel of the decade and among the ten best works of the genre ever authored—here, too, was a tale that would live on in ways few other writers imagined. Hence, the later Robert Heinlein verdict: "Final Blackout *is as perfect a piece of science fiction as has ever been written.*"

Portland, Oregon, 1943; L. Ron Hubbard, captain of the US Navy subchaser PC 815.

Like many another who both lived and wrote American pulp adventure, the war proved a tragic end to Ron's sojourn in the pulps. He served with distinction in four theaters and was highly decorated for commanding corvettes in the North Pacific. He was also grievously wounded in combat, lost many a close friend and colleague and thus resolved to say farewell to pulp fiction and devote himself to what it had supported these many years—namely, his serious research.

But in no way was the LRH literary saga at an end, for as he wrote some thirty years later, in 1980:

"Recently there came a period when I had little to do. This was novel in a life so crammed with busy years, and I decided to amuse myself by writing a novel that was pure *science fiction."*

That work was *Battlefield Earth: A Saga of the Year 3000*. It was an immediate *New York Times* bestseller and, in fact, the first international science fiction blockbuster in decades. It was not, however, L. Ron Hubbard's magnum opus, as that distinction is generally reserved for his next and final work: The 1.2 million word *Mission Earth*.

Final Blackout
is as perfect a piece of science fiction as has ever been written.
—Robert Heinlein

How he managed those 1.2 million words in just over twelve months is yet another piece of the L. Ron Hubbard legend. But the fact remains, he did indeed author a ten-volume *dekalogy* that lives in publishing history for the fact that each and every volume of the series was also a *New York Times* bestseller.

Moreover, as subsequent generations discovered L. Ron Hubbard through republished works and novelizations of his screenplays, the mere fact of his name on a cover signaled an international bestseller. . . . Until, to date, sales of his works exceed hundreds of millions, and he otherwise remains among the most enduring and widely read authors in literary history. Although as a final word on the tales of L. Ron Hubbard, perhaps it's enough to simply reiterate what editors told readers in the glory days of American Pulp Fiction:

He writes the way he does, brothers, because he's been there, seen it and done it!

THE STORIES FROM THE GOLDEN AGE

Your ticket to adventure starts here with the Stories from the Golden Age collection by master storyteller L. Ron Hubbard. These gripping tales are set in a kaleidoscope of exotic locales and brim with fascinating characters, including some of the most vile villains, dangerous dames and brazen heroes you'll ever get to meet.

The entire collection of over one hundred and fifty stories is being released in a series of eighty books and audiobooks. For an up-to-date listing of available titles, go to www.goldenagestories.com.

AIR ADVENTURE

Arctic Wings
The Battling Pilot
Boomerang Bomber
The Crate Killer
The Dive Bomber
Forbidden Gold
Hurtling Wings
The Lieutenant Takes the Sky
Man-Killers of the Air
On Blazing Wings
Red Death Over China
Sabotage in the Sky
Sky Birds Dare!
The Sky-Crasher
Trouble on His Wings
Wings Over Ethiopia

FAR-FLUNG ADVENTURE

The Adventure of "X"
All Frontiers Are Jealous
The Barbarians
The Black Sultan
Black Towers to Danger
The Bold Dare All
Buckley Plays a Hunch
The Cossack
Destiny's Drum
Escape for Three
Fifty-Fifty O'Brien
The Headhunters
Hell's Legionnaire
He Walked to War
Hostage to Death
Hurricane
The Iron Duke
Machine Gun 21,000
Medals for Mahoney
Price of a Hat
Red Sand
The Sky Devil
The Small Boss of Nunaloha
The Squad That Never Came Back
Starch and Stripes
Tomb of the Ten Thousand Dead
Trick Soldier
While Bugles Blow!
Yukon Madness

SEA ADVENTURE

Cargo of Coffins
The Drowned City
False Cargo
Grounded
Loot of the Shanung
Mister Tidwell, Gunner
The Phantom Patrol
Sea Fangs
Submarine
Twenty Fathoms Down
Under the Black Ensign

TALES FROM THE ORIENT

The Devil—With Wings
The Falcon Killer
Five Mex for a Million
Golden Hell
The Green God
Hurricane's Roar
Inky Odds
Orders Is Orders
Pearl Pirate
The Red Dragon
Spy Killer
Tah
The Trail of the Red Diamonds
Wind-Gone-Mad
Yellow Loot

MYSTERY

The Blow Torch Murder
Brass Keys to Murder
Calling Squad Cars!
The Carnival of Death
The Chee-Chalker
Dead Men Kill
The Death Flyer
Flame City
The Grease Spot
Killer Ape
Killer's Law
The Mad Dog Murder
Mouthpiece
Murder Afloat
The Slickers
They Killed Him Dead

FANTASY

Borrowed Glory
The Crossroads
Danger in the Dark
The Devil's Rescue
He Didn't Like Cats
If I Were You
The Last Drop
The Room
The Tramp

SCIENCE FICTION

The Automagic Horse
Battle of Wizards
Battling Bolto
The Beast
Beyond All Weapons
A Can of Vacuum
The Conroy Diary
The Dangerous Dimension
Final Enemy
The Great Secret
Greed
The Invaders
A Matter of Matter
The Obsolete Weapon
One Was Stubborn
The Planet Makers
The Professor Was a Thief
The Slaver
Space Can
Strain
Tough Old Man
240,000 Miles Straight Up
When Shadows Fall

WESTERN

The Baron of Coyote River
Blood on His Spurs
Boss of the Lazy B
Branded Outlaw
Cattle King for a Day
Come and Get It
Death Waits at Sundown
Devil's Manhunt
The Ghost Town Gun-Ghost
Gun Boss of Tumbleweed
Gunman!
Gunman's Tally
The Gunner from Gehenna
Hoss Tamer
Johnny, the Town Tamer
King of the Gunmen
The Magic Quirt
Man for Breakfast
The No-Gun Gunhawk
The No-Gun Man
The Ranch That No One Would Buy
Reign of the Gila Monster
Ride 'Em, Cowboy
Ruin at Rio Piedras
Shadows from Boot Hill
Silent Pards
Six-Gun Caballero
Stacked Bullets
Stranger in Town
Tinhorn's Daughter
The Toughest Ranger
Under the Diehard Brand
Vengeance Is Mine!
When Gilhooly Was in Flower